CR(

PHILIP RIDLEY was born in the East End of London. He studied painting at St Martin's School of Art. As well as three books for adults—and the highly acclaimed screenplay for the feature film *The Krays* (winner of the Evening Standard Best Film of the Year Award) —he has written many adult stage plays: the seminal *The Pitchfork Disney*, the multi-award-winning *The Fastest Clock in the Universe*, *Ghost from a Perfect Place*, *Vincent River*, *Mercury Fur*, *Leaves of Glass*, *Piranha Heights*, *Tender Napalm* (nominated for the London Fringe Best Play Award), *Shivered* (nominated for the Off-West End Best New Play Award), *Dark Vanilla Jungle* (winner of an Edinburgh Festival Fringe First Award), *Radiant Vermin*, *Tonight With Donny Stixx*, *Karagula* (nominated for the Off-West End Best New Play Award), *The Beast of Blue Yonder*, *The Poltergeist* (winner of the Off West End OnComm Award for Best Live Streamed Play), and *Tarantula*, plus several plays for young people: *Karamazoo*, *Fairytaleheart*, *Moonfleece* (named as one of the 50 Best Works about Cultural Diversity by the National Centre for Children's Books), *Sparkleshark* and *Brokenville*. He has also written books for children, including *Scribbleboy* (short-listed for the Carnegie Medal), *Kasper in the Glitter* (nominated for the Whitbread Prize), and the multi-award-winning bestseller *Krindlekrax*. He has also directed three feature films from his own screenplays: *The Reflecting Skin* (winner of eleven international awards, including the prestigious Georges Sadoul Prize), *The Passion of Darkly Noon* (winner of the Best Director Prize at the Porto Film Festival) and *Heartless* (winner of the Silver Mélièrs Award for Best Fantasy Film). In 2010 Philip, along with song-writing collaborator Nick Bicat, formed the music group Dreamskin Cradle and their first album, *Songs from Grimm*, is available on iTunes, Amazon and all major download sites. Philip is also a performance artist in his own right, and his highly-charged readings of his ongoing poetry sequence *Lovesongs for Extinct Creatures* (first embarked on when he was a student) have proved increasingly popular in recent years.

PHILIP RIDLEY

CROCODILIA

VALANCOURT BOOKS

Crocodilia by Philip Ridley
Originally published in a different form in Great Britain by
Brilliance Books in 1988
This fully revised edition first published 2021

The right of Philip Ridley to be identified as Author of this work
has been asserted by him in accordance with the Copyright,
Designs and Patents Act 1988.

Published by Valancourt Books, Richmond, Virginia
http://www.valancourtbooks.com

ISBN 978-1-948405-92-8 (hardcover)
ISBN 978-1-948405-93-5 (trade paperback)

Sex and stories are very similar:
they both require feeling,
and a climax.

William Corvus

PROLOGUE

THIS IS A STORY ABOUT CROCODILES. It's about other things as well, of course. But, mostly, there are crocodiles.

When I was a child my mum used to tell me bedtime stories. I would snuggle up to her – my lips still sticky and sweet with cocoa – and listen to her create narrative spells with the ease of a necromancer.

Mum never read from a book. The stories she told me were *her* stories, *her* creations. In these tales she always had a princess. The princess would have red hair and blue eyes, the same as Mum. The same as me.

In one of the fairy tales a princess fell in love with a star (the celestial – not silver screen – kind). In another, a princess walked a hundred miles to pick (and eat) a nectarine from The End of Unhappiness Tree. I don't remember if the love the princess felt for the star was ever reciprocated, or if eating the nectarine made the other princess eternally joyful. In fact, I don't remember the *whole* story of *anything* Mum told me. All I have are fragments, odd images: a king who wore a golden cloak that made people adore him, a garden that blossomed with love letters from imaginary lovers, a prince weeping in the middle of a jungle.

My family lived in the East End of London. In Bethnal Green. Both my parents had been born there (as had their parents (as had their parents)). Mum and Dad were married in the local church, St Peter's (nicknamed the Red Church, because of the colour of its bricks), and then got a flat in the newly built Bradley Estate. The Estate – with its concrete geometrics, and balconies of frosted glass – was initially considered, at least according to the publicity brochure, 'a forward-thinking place for the families of tomorrow', but, within five years, it had become – to use Mum's words – 'a graffiti-covered dump.' I grew up listening to Mum say how she wanted to move out and get a house with a garden, but with Dad's health never good (he had his first heart attack at twenty-one), and with a couple of children to look after (my sister, Anne, then me a few years later), there was barely enough money to pay the rent, let alone *buy* a property.

When I was thirteen I dreamt this: my cock was dangling between my legs like the tail of some gigantic lizard. I pulled it up to my lips and stretched the foreskin back to expose the splendid helmet. It was smooth and gleaming. I licked the tip of my cock and felt my whole body tingle with a storm of electric shocks. I started to rub my cock until it was hard, like a tusk in silk.

I became aware of a shadowy presence standing behind me. I could feel their breath on my neck. They whispered in my ear, 'Shall I help you with that.'

'Yes,' I said.

The shadowy figure stood beside me. He – for, though shadowy, the figure was definitely male (I sensed his gender rather than saw it) – started to rub my penis.

He asked, 'Do you like that?'

'Yes.'

Suddenly I ejaculated, pumping bucket loads of steaming spunk over both myself and the stranger. The sperm covered us and set hard like aspic, trapping us inside separate cocoons. The surface of our cocoons was rough and scaly, like the skin of some reptile. I could just about make out the shadowy figure inside his chrysalis, just as – presumably – he could just about make out me. Both of us were pushing and struggling to be free. Finally, our cocoons split open, and we emerged, glistening with ooze, like newborn things.

I wanted to kiss the shadowy figure's face. But I woke up before I had a chance.

In a way, the story I want to tell begins there. The night when I had my first wet dream and woke before I kissed my lover's face. So we'll say – for the sake of convenience – that the story has already begun. Although nothing much will happen for another five years.

For five years I slept . . . waiting for crocodiles.

PART ONE

CHAPTER ONE

'You can't keep saying, "Oh, I need to find myself",
and then – '

'I *don't* keep saying – '

'Okay! So they're *my* words. But it's what you *mean*.
"Oh, I wish I had some freedom!" "Oh, I wish my life
was differ – " '

'Okay, okay.'

'Well, stop *moaning* about it and – '

'*Do* something. I know, I – '

'You need to be more – '

'Proactive.'

'Exactly!'

'I *want* to be!'

'*Prove* it!' Anne grabbed my arm. 'Move in *here*, Dom!
Say yes. *Now!* Don't overthink things like you always do.'

'I *don't* overthink things . . . *Do* I?'

It was the summer of 1982 (the first Monday in
August) and I'd gone round to see my sister, Anne, in
the house she'd moved into (the previous year) with her
husband, Darryl. It was an old (*very* old), red-bricked,
mid-terraced building, with moss-covered chimneys,
cracked walls, and – in some rooms – defunct gas-light
fittings from the turn of the century.

Anne had asked me to move in with her and Darryl
once before – as soon as I'd turned eighteen, back in
March – and I almost did (I'd even picked what one – of

the two – spare rooms I wanted), but then . . . I changed my mind. Or, as Anne would say, 'overthought things'.

'Mum won't like it,' I said. 'Me living here.'

'Oh, we've had this discussion a million times. There's *nothing* you can do – nothing any of us can *ever* do – that'll make Mum happy. You *know* that.'

'I know but –'

'Mum thrives on being let down. It's where she gets her energy.'

'I know but –'

'Listen! You do *not* want to be living at home when you start art school next month. What if you meet someone you fancy? Would you be able to ask them back to stay the night? No!'

'I'm not going to art school just to *meet* someone, Anne.'

'Well, you *should* be. It's about *time* you – Oh, *don't* do that, Liam!'

Liam, Anne's toddler son, had thrown one of his toy cars across the room.

'Why must boys break their toys?' Anne said.

'I didn't break *my* toys.'

'You broke my dolls.'

'I just . . . "enhanced" them.'

'You cut off their hair and painted their faces gold!'

'And much better they looked for it too.'

'I should've kept them. They'll probably be worth a fortune when you're a world-famous artist.' She held my hand. '*Do* it, Dom! Make your wish come true. Live *here! Change* things!'

CHAPTER TWO

'You're doing *what?!*'

'Moving in with Anne.'

'You're joking *surely.*'

'Does it *look* like I'm joking, Mum?' I took my note-books from the bedside cabinet and started putting them into one of the large sports bags (belonging to Darryl) that Anne had loaned me. The other bag – out in the hall-way – was already full of my clothes (all of them black: Mum's oft-said quip was, 'Whose funeral you going to?').

'But . . . but . . .' Mum looked like all the oxygen was being sucked out of the room and she still had a few arias to belt out, '. . . when was all this decided?'

'This afternoon.'

'Without talking to *me* first?'

'It's for the best.'

'For *who?*'

'Everyone.'

'Not for *me!* Your sister lives so far away. I'll never see you.'

'She lives in *Bow*, Mum. It's a couple of miles away at the most.'

'It's not the distance in *miles* I'm talking about.' She clutched at my (now empty) beside cabinet as if she was about to faint (old Hollywood melodramas were in her DNA). 'And how can you even *think* about living in the same house as that . . . that . . . I don't even want to say the man's name.'

The unsaid name was – who else? – Darryl. He and Anne had met when she was almost eighteen and he had just turned twenty-one. Mum didn't like him from the start. And that's putting it mildly.

I picked up my portable typewriter.

'We bought you that for your fourteenth birthday,' Mum said. 'Remember?'

'Of *course* I remember.'

'Your Dad and me always thought you were going to Oxford to study writing.'

'It wasn't to study "writing", Mum,' I said, squeezing the typewriter into the bag. 'It was to study English Language and Literature.'

'Whatever it was, you passed that special exam you needed to get in.'

'No, Mum. I passed the "special exam" I needed to get an *interview* to –'

'And *then* what happens? Out of the blue, it's *art school* you want to go to.'

'Hardly out of the bloody blue.' I pointed at the paintings, drawings and photographs on the wall. 'Who did all these, I wonder? Hang on! *I* did.' I took one of the photos down. A Polaroid of myself taken on my eighteenth birthday.

'Your dad took that,' Mum said.

'*I* took it, Mum.'

'Who takes photographs of themselves!?'

'*Artists* do! It's called a self-portraiture.' I put the photo on top of the typewriter. 'I'll come back for the rest of my stuff another time.'

Mum said, 'You know what you've done to me, don't you? Exactly what your sister did. You've turned into someone I don't know anymore.'

'Mum –'

'Your dad will probably have another heart attack when he finds out you've gone.'

'Don't pull *that* guilt trip on me, Mum! It's not fair!'

'He could die at any time!'

'We *all* could!'

'Stay until he gets home from work *at least!*'

'Mum – '

'Oh, just *go* if you're going! What're you bloody waiting for?' She swept out of the room (I don't need to say with 'a melodramatic flourish' but – hell! – I just have) and went to the kitchen, where she started rattling pots and pans with such persistence and volume you'd think she was writing a concerto for percussion.

I thought, *I should go to her. I should hug her. I should tell her I love her.*

But I didn't.

CHAPTER THREE

'The sky will be a different sky
The sun will shine like new.'

I was in my room at Anne's – putting my typewriter on the desk – when the music started.

It was coming from the house next door: someone was strumming a guitar and –

> *'You'll see yourself,*
> *you'll hear yourself,*
> *and wonder, "Is that me?"'*

The singer was in the upstairs back room of his house, the same as me, so we were only separated by a brick wall and, on my side at least, layer upon layer of wallpaper (some of which was so old it resembled parchment from a medieval manuscript).

The voice was clear and strong, yet somehow broken. Like a heartache in damaged armour.

> *'You'll feel a rainbow in your heart*
> *and want everyone to see it.'*

Anne breezed in carrying a cup of tea and a sandwich. 'Thought you might like a late night snack.'
'Thanks – Can you hear that?' I asked.

'What?'

'Singing . . . It's stopped now.'

Anne put the tea and sandwich on the bedside cabinet, and then looked round the room. 'Well, it's starting to look *very* cosy in here already.'

'Yeah,' I said. 'It'll feel more like home when I get some bookshelves up.'

'Darryl'll sort those out when he gets back. And anything else you need.'

Darryl drove a delivery van for a local furniture company. He'd got the job soon after he and Anne were married, and initially – at his request – only delivered locally in case Anne – who was pregnant at the time – should need him. But, for the past year, he'd been doing – again, at his request – more and more long distance work (mostly to Scotland and Northern Ireland, but a few times to France) – because it paid more (much more), and he and Anne needed every penny they could get to finish decorating the house.

When Anne and I had discussed me moving in previously, Darryl had got some furniture from work ('At a hundred per cent discount,' Darryl assured me, which I took to mean it had all fallen off the back of a lorry), so that's why I already had a bed, desk and bedside cabinet.

'Where *is* Darryl?' I asked. 'Shouldn't he be home by now?'

Anne nodded. 'He must've got caught in traffic. It happens a lot.' She kissed my cheek. 'I'm having an early night. Liam's been exhausting today.' She squeezed my hand. 'I'm glad you're here.'

'So am I.'

Anne went to her room

The singing from next door started again.

'I am the change you want to be.
So be it, be it, be it.
I am the change you want to see.
So see it, see it, see it.'

I went to the window. The strumming of the guitar got louder. The stranger next door was so close that – if the wall wasn't there – I could reach out and touch him.

CHAPTER FOUR

I was digging weeds in the garden when I heard someone come out of the house next door.

It must be the singer from last night!

The wooden fence between our houses was –
although splintered and full of holes – so covered with
ivy, clematis, and roses (amongst other climbing ten-
drils), that it was difficult to see anything on the other
side.

I tried to prise some foliage apart, but thorns – and an
angry wasp – got the better of me.

He's walking in his garden.

I crept along the length of the fence, peering through
the undergrowth, hoping for any glimpse of –

I spotted a gap in the foliage and fence.

I peered through.

He was wearing a green T-shirt (ripped in places),
green jeans (very tight, and torn round the knees), and
his arms were covered with tattoos –

'Hello,' he said.

Is he talking to me?

'You!' he said again. 'Next door!'

'Oh . . . hello,' I said, trying to sound as casual as possible.

'I think I've found something that might be yours.'
His hand came through the (letterbox-sized) gap in
the foliage. It had golden rings on every finger. Most of

them were decorated with bright green jewels. He was holding a toy gold Cadillac. '*Is* it yours?'

'Yes. Well, it's Liam's. My nephew. He's got lots of toy cars. My dad gets them for him. Dad works at Lesney's.'

'Lesney's?'

'The factory down by the Hackney stadium. It makes Matchbox toys. Tiny cars. Dad works on the assembly line. If any of the toy cars get to the end of the assembly line in a "not sales perfect" condition the workers are allowed to take them home.'

I was aware I was talking too much – jabbering! – but I couldn't seem to stop.

'Dad used to bring cars home for me when I was younger. But I was never really into cars. Not to play with. I used to *draw* them. My sister – *she* used to play with them. She's *still* interested in cars. She wants to start taking driving lessons as soon as – '

'Are you going to take the car?'

'Oh. Yes. Sorry.'

I took the Cadillac, making sure I touched the stranger's palm in the process.

His skin's so cool.

I would have risked any number of thorns and stings to touch him for longer, but his hand (and arm) withdrew. But not before I got a better look at the tattoos.

'Crocodiles!' I said. 'On your arm.'

'I've got one on my back too. A big one. Would you like to see it?'

'Yeah!' I said (not sounding casual at all).

I peered (as close as I dare) through the thorns and wasps.

His hair's green!

And it was shaven at the sides, Mohican style.

A punk!

He looked a year or so older than me.

He was pulling his T-shirt up . . . up . . . His skin was smooth and ghostly pale.

I caught a glimpse of his navel, and then his nipples, before he turned to reveal his back.

A tattoo of a crocodile ran down the length of his spine, its jaws up by his neck, its tail disappearing behind his leather belt and into the cleavage of his buttocks.

'It's . . . wonderful,' I said.

'If I move . . . it comes alive. Watch!'

He flexed some muscles.

The crocodile appeared to crawl.

My cock had never got so hard, so quick.

'Show over!' He pulled his T-shirt back down. 'Bye.'

He started walking back towards his house –

'*I* was thinking of getting a tattoo!' I blurted out.

Why did I say that?

He stopped and turned round. 'Oh, *really*?' He stepped closer. 'Of *what* exactly?'

'Oh . . . I don't know. I . . . I just like the idea.'

'You "just like the *idea*?" '

I'm making a fool of myself.

'Yes,' I said. 'Perhaps . . . perhaps I'll get a crocodile. Like yours. A small one. On my arm or . . . some place. I don't know – Phew! It's getting hotter. They say we're going to have a heatwave. Do you like hot weather? I don't. My perfect weather is when it's bright, but chilly. Fresh. October weather . . . Sorry. I'm talking too much.'

'. . . What's your name?' he asked.

'Dominic.'

'Okay . . . See you around, Dom.' He started walking towards his house again.

'What's *your* name?' I found myself calling.

'Billy Crow!'

The back door slammed shut behind him and –

I ran into the house. I ran through the kitchen. I ran up the stairs, dropping the gold Cadillac and unbuckling my jeans along the way. By the time I got to my room, I was pulling my jeans down and reaching inside my boxer shorts. I half fell – half threw myself – onto the bed, and started frantically rubbing my cock –

A guitar being tuned!

Billy's in his room!

His window, like mine, must've been wide open for me to be hearing him so clearly.

If I can hear him . . . then he can hear me.

I wanted him to hear me!

I gasped even louder, writhing on the bed, thrusting my cock into my fist and –

The guitar stopped tuning.

He's listening to me!

I jerked and writhed so hard that the headboard started slam-slamming against the wall. I didn't want him in any doubt as to what I was doing.

Listen to this, Billy!

Listen!

Suddenly, every atom of my skin split and glowed like a supernova, and my body started convulsing as –

'I'm cumming!' I cried. 'I'm . . . cum –'

I'm standing in the centre of a candlelit stone room. My body is encrusted with a galaxy of jewels: emeralds running down my spine, sapphires and diamonds across my forehead, rubies on my chest. My fingernails are covered with gold leaf. My anus is stretched with sapphires and amethyst. I glitter and glimmer in the candlelight. I am staring through a small window.

Outside . . . it's snowing.

CHAPTER FIVE

This is the story of how Mum discovered God.

One day, shortly after my fourteenth birthday, I came home from school, took off my uniform, then sat at the desk in my room to type up a short story I'd written (on the very typewriter I'm using now).

> When the Prince was born
> the Queen said, 'My child is the most
> beautiful thing in the whole yniverzx'

I hadn't been using the typewriter for very long, so I was still getting used to the keys (and all its other machinations).

I got some Tippex correction fluid and painted over the misspelt word, then typed 'universe' on top.

'You should have some typing lessons.'

Anne was standing in the doorway. She'd just got home from school and was still clutching her satchel (which looked heavy with homework).

'I don't <u>need</u> typing lessons,' I said.

'Zoë can teach you. She's sixty words a minute.'

Zoë was Anne's best friend.

'I don't <u>want</u> Zoë to teach me. Besides, it's not <u>all</u> about speed. As Truman Capote said about some third-rate novelist, 'It's typing, but it's not writing.'

'Jack Kerouac.'

'Eh?'

'<u>That</u> was the novelist. Hardly third rate - What're you looking at me like for? You're not the only one who's read a book around here, you know.'

The phone in the hallway started to ring.

'I'll get it,' Anne said. 'You finish your masterpiece.'

I heard Anne answer the phone and say, 'Hello, Mum . . . Yes . . . Yes . . . I understand.'

There was something about the tone of her voice that made me get up and go to the hallway.

Anne put the phone down and looked at me. 'Dad was taken ill at work. Mum's with him at the hospital. They think it's another heart attack. Mum wants us both there.'

I don't remember the bus ride to London Hospital (or entering the building, or the long walk down corridor after corridor), but I do remember seeing Dad lying in bed, with tubes coming out of his arms and his mouth, and thinking, I don't want to be here.

Anne kissed Dad and said, 'I love you, Dad.'

I wondered how she knew what to do? Had she read a manual?

Mum looked at me and said, 'Why don't you wait outside, love.'

I walked out of the ward and sat in the corridor.

How long was I there? A minute? An hour?

Anne came out of the ward and told me there was 'no change', and that Mum had said I could go home if I wanted to.

I did, so I did.

I went straight to my room and, basically, that's where I stayed for ... how many days? Three? Four?

I was vaguely aware of Mum and Anne coming and going, and – at some point – the word 'surgery' being mentioned, and – at another – the phrase 'might kill him', but I was too engrossed with my writing and drawing to let any of it bother me too much.

And then I was aware of Mum coming home and ... a new voice! A man.

I got up from my desk and walked down the hallway. The man's voice got louder ... louder –

'This is my son!' Mum said, seeing me hovering at the living room door. She indicated a man sitting on the sofa. 'Dominic, this is Father Leonard.'

Father Leonard got to his feet and held his hand out. 'So you're the artistic one of the family, are you?'

I didn't say anything. I shook his hand.

Father Leonard was about fifty years old, and had the hair of a sergeant major, the voice of a newscaster, and the neck of a struggling weightlifter.

'I must say,' Father Leonard said, 'it surprised me – nay, troubled me! – that you didn't visit your dad at the hospital. This isn't his first heart attack, is it?'

Mum piped up with, 'It's his second, Father.'
She nodded in my direction. 'He knows that.'

'That's a very serious thing, Dominic. Few
people survive <u>one</u> heart attack, let alone <u>two</u>.
Your dad needed you by his side. We must honour
our parents, Dominic.'

I wondered why Mum was letting him talk to me
like this?

'But God has blessed your dad, Dominic,'
Father Leonard went on. 'The operation has
been a complete success . . . Were you even aware
he was <u>having</u> an operation?'

'I was aware, yes,' I said.

Why wasn't Mum telling him to shut up and
leave me alone?

Father Leonard went on, 'I hope you will now
visit your dad, Dominic, and tell him that you
love him. Will you do that?'

'Of course, yeah.'

'Good, good. Now, I must be on my way. I shall
see myself out.' He held Mum's hand. 'We shall see
each other again at church, Marian. Yes?'

'Of course, Father.'

When the front door had closed, Mum said,
'I don't know what I would have done without
Father Leonard. I've been in the loneliest
place of my life and he . . . he showed me a way
out of it. He told me to pray. And I did. I said
to God, "If you save my husband, I will be yours
forever."'

CHAPTER SIX

'ARE YOU THERE?'

I opened my eyes.

'DOM!? ARE YOU THERE?!'

It was the day after I talked to Billy in the garden. I'd slept late because I'd been up until the small hours drawing and writing, and – when I did eventually start to drift off – I was disturbed by Darryl coming home from work.

I was vaguely aware of Anne telling me earlier that she and Darryl were taking Liam to the park. (Darryl had been given the day off work as he'd had two late nights in a row.) Anne had asked if I wanted to join them. I'd mumbled a groggy negative, and then went back to sleep.

'DOM?'

'YEAH!' I jumped out of bed. 'I'm here, I'm here!' I looked out of the window, squinting against the sunshine.

Billy was leaning out of his window.

'Morning,' I said.

'Afternoon.'

'*Is* it?'

'Just gone midday. How can you sleep in this heat? My bed was wet with sweat. Look at me!'

He was stripped to the waist. He ran a hand over his gleaming chest and stomach. He licked the sweat from his fingers. 'Very salty,' he said. 'Want to taste it?'

'I can't reach from here.'

'So . . . will you come *here* or shall I come *there*?'

'*I'll* come *there*.'

'I'll be waiting – Oh! Nearly forgot! Have you got a camera?'

'I've got a Polaroid.'

'Any film?

'One shot left, I think.'

'One's all I need.'

I washed and dressed as quickly as possible, grabbed the Polaroid camera, and then rushed next door.

Billy's front door didn't have a number. In its place there was a drawing of a crocodile.

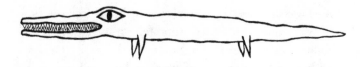

I knocked.

'It's open!' I heard Billy call.

I went inside.

The hallway, like Anne's, had layer upon layer of paper on the walls, but – unlike Anne's – there was no carpet on the floor, nor any sign of furniture.

'I'm upstairs, Dom!'

'Okay!'

Billy's house was the mirror image of the one I was living in. So instead of going up the stairs and turning right into my room, I went up the stairs and turned left into Billy's.

'Welcome,' he said.

There was a mattress on the floor, an old table covered with cans of spray paint, and a wardrobe. Two of the walls had been covered with paintings of –

'Crocodiles!' I said.

'Of course,' Billy said, smiling. 'I can't live anywhere without crocodiles.'

They were disconcertingly three-dimensional, and ablaze with colour (shades of viridian flecked with amber for the epidermis, cadmium red – with ruby rhinestones – for the eyes, and glittering gold for the claws).

'They're amazing!' I said. I looked closer. 'You've painted on top of the old wallpaper?'

Billy nodded. 'The crinkled texture makes it look more like crocodile skin.'

'How long did it take you to do all this?'

'Not long. I only moved in here the day before yester-day.'

'That's when I moved in with my sister.'

'What a coincidence – Aha! The Polaroid!'

I gave it to him. 'I'm not sure the quality of a Polaroid will do justice to your painting.'

'I'm not taking a photo of the painting.'

'What d'you want it for, then?'

'You'll see. Fancy a Coke?'

'That would be great.'

'Here.' He handed me a bottle. 'It's not cold. No fridge. I haven't managed to get the electric working yet. Squatting is cheap, but there are *some* drawbacks.'

'How do you paint at night?'

'I use that.' He pointed at a golden candelabrum in the corner. 'I prefer candlelight anyway. It makes the crocodiles come alive!' He raised his Coke. 'Cheers.'

'Cheers.'

It was the first time I'd seen his eyes up close. They were bright green. Like sunlight through spring leaves.

I looked at the crocodiles again. 'I love the gold on their claws.'

'It's gold leaf.'

'You can't afford to pay *rent*, but you can afford *gold leaf*?'

'I only spend money on things that *really* matter.' He ran his fingers over his smooth, flat stomach.

'I'd *love* to do a painting with gold leaf,' I said. 'Is it difficult?'

'Not really. Just fiddly. I'll show you how, if you like.'

'Oh, I . . . I'd *love* that. I'm going to St Martin's School of Art in September and –'

'No, no!'

' "No, no" *what*?'

'Don't tell me.'

'About going to St Martin's?'

'About *anything*. I don't want to know *anything* about you. The only thing that matters is what happens here – now! – with us.' He took a step towards me. 'There is no "what I did before". There is no "what I'll do in the future".' Another step closer. 'All that matters is us. In this room full of crocodiles. As E. M. Forster said, "Only connect . . . to crocodiles." '

'That's not *quite* what he said.'

Billy grinned. 'Well, it *should've* been.'

I can feel the heat of him.

'Do you want to taste it now?' he asked.

'Taste what?'

'My sweat.'

'Oh . . . yeah.'

He ran his fingers over his chest and neck, slowly, until they were gleaming, then he brought them up to my lips. 'Open,' he said.

I opened my mouth.

'Head back.'

I held my head back.

I felt a drop of sweat land on my tongue.

The saline sparkled through my whole body.

I felt a little giddy, so I reached out for him, my hands sliding round his waist.

Oh, his skin!

He reached out for me too, pulling me closer.

We're going to kiss!

I wanted this to happen more than anything.

I was scared of this happening more than –

We kissed!

His tongue started nuzzling between my lips, my teeth, touching my tongue and –

Flash!

The Polaroid camera.

He's taken a photo of us!

The photo slid out of the camera.

'Wh-what're you doing?' I asked, pulling away.

'A photograph of the first time we kissed,' he said, stepping back. 'I like to have a record of such things.'

'How many records of "such things" have you got?'

Billy grinned. 'Jealous already?' He started to flap the photo in the air. 'I've never found out if all this agitation really *does* help Polaroids develop but . . . well, everyone seems to do it.'

'You're supposed to put them somewhere dark too.'

'Really?' His grin grew wider. 'I know just the place.' He unbuckled his jeans, slid the photo behind the waistband of his boxer shorts, and then down into his crotch. 'Want to . . . agitate the photo for me?'

I put my hand on the cock bulge of his jeans.

I started to rub my hand up and down.

'That's it,' he said. 'Oh, yes . . . yes . . . I can feel it developing.'

I rubbed faster and faster.

I could feel his cock getting harder . . . harder . . .

Billy started moaning and gasping, thrusting his hips rhythmically forward. 'Oh, yes . . . yes . . .'

I'd been fantasizing about having a sexual experience with another man for years, and now –

This is actually happening!

This is actually –

'Faster!' Billy said.

I looked at his stomach muscles tensing. His rib cage expanding. His pubic hair, pearled with sweat, peeking more and more above his underwear. There was so much to see. Too much. Like trying to look at every spark in a firework display.

This is actually happening!

This is actually happening!

This is –

'I'm cumming!' Billy gasped.

A cyclone of air gushed from his lungs.

He leant against me for a moment, his breath furnacing my neck.

Slowly, he stood up straight, put his hand down his boxer shorts, and pulled out the photo.

It was lustrous with spunk.

'Perfect!' Billy showed it to me. 'What do you think?'

I was still submerged in an ocean of arousal. I found it hard to breathe, let alone speak.

'Oh, look at you,' Billy said. 'You're still turned on.' He whispered in my ear. 'Next time *I'll* make *you* come. Promise!'

CHAPTER SEVEN

'The night feels as hot as the day,' I said.

'Mmm,' Darryl said.

'Hard to sleep when it's like this.'

'Mmm.'

We were both sitting in the garden, picking at the remains of the pizzas Darryl and Anne had bought on their way back from the park.

The sun had set. I could see stars.

It was the longest I'd ever been alone with Darryl, and to say I was struggling to make conversation is like saying the Arctic can get a bit chilly.

It's nine hours since I made Billy cum.

I said, 'At least you're out in the fresh air all day, not cooped up in an office.'

'Mmm.'

'And I bet you see some interesting places.'

'Not really.'

'But Anne said you've been to France a few times. That must've been – '

'It was boring. Okay? My job is boring. I sit in a boring delivery truck all day, driving down boring motorways to boring places where I meet boring people.' He took a big gulp from his can of lager. 'Nothing "interesting" ever happens to me.'

From inside the house Liam started yelling, 'MUM! . . . MUM! . . . MUM!'

Anne had put Liam to bed soon after they'd all got

back. Or, rather, she'd *tried* to put him to bed. I knew from what Anne had told me before – and what I'd seen since I'd been living there – getting Liam to go to sleep wasn't the easiest thing in the world.

It's nine hours and seven minutes since I made Billy cum.

I said, 'Should . . . one of us go up and help?'

'By "one of us" you mean *me*?'

'Well, Anne's been coping with it all evening and I just thought – '

'Anne's the only one who *can* cope with it.' He opened another lager, glancing at me. 'Oh, I know what you're thinking. "Poor Anne. She was studying for her A-levels, had a wonderful career ahead of her, and then stupid ol' Darryl comes along and ruins it all." '

'Darryl, I'm sorry if I – '

'Well, *I* had plans too, you know.' He gulped some lager. 'I'd been spotted by a model scout the week before I met Anne. I was going to New York to do a shoot for *Vogue*. Did you *know* that?'

'No.'

'Of *course* you didn't. Why? Because you – like everyone else in this fucking family – never ask me *anything* about *me*.'

'I'm asking *now*, Darryl. What happened?'

He finished the can of lager and opened another one. His seventh in the past two hours. Anne had told me Darryl 'liked his drink'. This was the first time I'd seen just *how* much he liked it.

Darryl said, 'I was working on my Uncle Ernie's stall. It was a hot day. Bloody hot. Like today. Only this was in early April. Freak heatwave. I was a bit nervous about taking my shirt off because I hadn't had a chance to build up a decent tan. But then I thought, "What the hell!" A gulp of lager. 'I saw someone looking at me. A woman.

She looked a bit posh. She wasn't buying anything. Just standing there and . . . gawping. I didn't mind. Women were gawping at me all the time. Tan or no tan. I had a good body then.'

'You've got a good body *now*.'

Why did I say that?!

'Not like I had *then*.' He finished his can of lager and threw it to the bottom of the garden. 'People used to tell me I had the body of a matador. Did you know that? Of course you didn't.' He gazed at the garden, as if seeing his teenaged self strutting amongst the ruined shed and broken terracotta pots.

'What about the woman?' I asked.

'Eh? . . . Oh!' He opened another can. 'She comes over and says she works for a modelling agency. A famous one. In Mayfair.' Gulp. 'She said it was her job to find people who had the potential to be world-famous models. "And you," she said to me, "have *lots* of potential."' Gulp.

It's nine hours and ten minutes since I made Billy cum.

I look up at Billy's window.

I can see candlelight.

And then I hear –

> '*The touch of him, the heat of him,*
> *The pulse and beat and breath of him.*'

Darryl went on, 'The woman gave me her card. She said, "If you're interested, give me a call." Well, I *was* interested. So I *did* give her a call. The very next day, in fact. The woman said she'd like to set me up with a photographer friend of hers. To get some portfolio shots.' Gulp. 'We set a date for the following week. The woman said, "Trust me, you'll be in New York doing the front cover of *Vogue* by the summer. And *do* try to get a bit of a tan. You'll be taking your shirt off." '

> *'The sound of him, the sight of him,*
> *The dreaming through the night with him.'*

'My Uncle Ernie – oh, he was over the moon about me becoming a model. He said to me, "You deserve some luck in your life." He gave me an extra bit of pocket money to go to the seaside and do some sunbathing that weekend. "Get that tan you need for the photos," he said. Uncle Ernie . . . he'd been like a dad to me since my real dad fucked off. I don't know what I would have done without my Uncle Ernie . . . no one else cared about me . . . only Uncle . . . Ernie . . .' Tears started to trickle down Darryl's face. He wiped them away. 'Anyway, the rest you already know.' Gulp, gulp. 'I went to Southend, met your sister on the beach and – POW! Soon as I saw her, nothing else existed.'

> *'The eyes of him, the hands of him,*
> *The always answered wish of him.'*

Darryl said, 'Uncle Ernie kept telling me, "Don't forget the photo session!" And I kept saying, "Of *course* I won't forget." But, of course, I did. Or, perhaps, I just didn't want to remember. Because I certainly did *not* want to go all the way to New York – for fuck knows how long – and be away from Anne. Uncle Ernie – he hit the bloody roof. He said, "You're being led by your cock, Darryl! Don't let this girl ruin your life. Phone up that scout woman. Ask her to give you a second chance." I said I would. But I didn't.' He drained his can of lager. 'And then Anne got pregnant . . . and . . .' He crushed the

empty can in his fist and then threw it into the foliage.
'Fuck it!' He got to his feet and looked down at me. 'I
could be a world-famous model living in the Big Apple
by now,' he said. 'But instead ... I'm a nothing living
nowhere. I need to piss.' He went into the house.

*It's nine hours and nineteen minutes since I made Billy
cum.*

I could see Billy's shadow inside his room, moving
about and playing the guitar.

> *'Oh, let me live my life with him.*
> *Thought to thought,*
> *Skin to skin.*
> *A universe of*
> *Me and him.'*

CHAPTER EIGHT

This is the story of how Mum got a job at the Rex.

The finest cinema in the East End of London, certainly the most luxurious, was - and to some extent still is - the Rex down Bethnal Green Road.

An art deco building, painted pale pistachio, with gilt curlicue trimmings wherever they would fit (and sometimes where they wouldn't), the cinema was considered to be 'an entertainment wonderland'. At least, that's what the East London Chronicle called it in an article dated 16th August 1957.

The reason I know what the local newspaper had said about the Rex all those years ago (indeed the reason I can recite most of the article by heart) is that a clipping of it had been kept in the top drawer of my mum's dressing table.

Why?

The article contained a photograph of the staff who worked at the Rex. They were all raising champagne glasses and smiling very hard. One of the ushers, third from the left, was 'chief usherette, Marian Loomis'. My mum.

When Mum was younger - before she met my

dad – she and her mum (my Grandmother Harriet, who died before I was born) would often go to the cinema together. They were both big fans of Joan Crawford and Bette Davis (a passion I share), so when Johnny Guitar (the new Joan Crawford) came to the Rex (in 1954), they decided to make a night of it, and have a fish supper beforehand at Pellicci's, the café nearby.

Mum was hoping that this 'girls' night out' would put her mum in better spirits. Grandmother Harriet hadn't been quite herself for several months. She was constantly tired, had frequent chills, and suffered from night sweats that left her drained and nauseous. Despite these symptoms, Mum was convinced the root of Grandmother Harriet's problems were psychological rather than physical (Grandmother Harriet had suffered from bouts of depression ever since her husband – my Granddad Percy – had been killed at Dunkirk in 1940), so what better remedy to banish the blues than a fish and chips supper, followed by Joan Crawford dressed up like a cowboy?

Mum and Grandmother Harriet bought a box of Dairy Milk chocolates at the Rex's confectionery kiosk, and then rushed up to the front row of the circle (their favourite seats).

They'd only eaten a couple of chocolates – and Joan Crawford had only made the briefest of appearances – when Mum became aware of Grandmother Harriet swaying strangely in her seat.

'Are you feeling all right, Mum?' she asked.

Grandmother Harriet whispered, 'I'm feeling

a little ... not quite myself. I think I should ...'
And started to get, uneasily, to her feet.

Mum helped Grandmother Harriet as best
she could (difficult with a full row, and with
Grandmother Harriet refusing to let go of the
box of Dairy Milk). They'd almost made it out of
the auditorium when Grandmother Harriet fell
to her knees. A couple of men sitting in the row
nearby jumped up and helped Mum escort Grandmother Harriet down to the foyer.

'There's no need to worry,' Mum informed the
men. 'Mum often has funny turns like this.'

That's when Grandmother Harriet passed out
altogether, dropping the box of Dairy Milk,
scattering chocolates everywhere.

Some of the Rex's ushers were now appearing
(clearly flustered), and several people who'd
followed Mum and Grandmother Harriet out of
the auditorium were hovering nearby.

'Please, everyone, don't make a fuss,' Mum
said. 'This will all be over in a jiffy ... There!
She's coming around already? Can you stand up,
Mum? ... That's it. Help me put her in a chair
someone, please.'

Grandmother Harriet was sat in a chair.

Mum said, 'Could someone open the doors so
Mum gets some air, please? Could someone get
Mum a glass of water, please? Could someone get
a magazine so Mum can fan herself, please?'

The doors were opened, the glass of water
brought, and a copy of **Film Review** Monthly was
put into Grandmother Harriet's hand.

'There!' Mum said. 'Mum's on her way to recov-
ery. Aren't you, Mum?'

Grandmother Harriet nodded.

Mum said to those people who'd left the auditorium, 'Please go back and enjoy the film. I'd hate this to spoil your evening in any way ... That's it. And thank you for your concern, everyone. Now, let me clear this mess up.' She dutifully picked up every dropped Dairy Milk chocolate and threw them, and the box, away.

Coming down the stairs while all this had been going on was the cinema's manager, Major Vernon (the 'Major' was more nickname than official title). He was wearing a dark blue, shot-silk suit, cravat, highly polished brogues, and had a thick mop of brunette hair, and matinée idol smile. Rumour had it he'd been recruited by the Secret Service while still an undergraduate at Cambridge, and had gone on to foil countless enemy plots during the Second World War. A very dashing story for a very dapper man.

Major Vernon did what he could to help, but mainly he watched, impressed by the way this young woman, my mum, dealt with the whole situation.

Grandmother Harriet, after ten minutes or so, was back to her old self, and feeling terribly embarrassed about all the trouble she'd caused. 'It must have been the fish we ate earlier,' she said. 'I thought it smelt a bit off.'

'It was probably the sight of Joan Crawford in a Western,' Mum said with a chuckle.

'Yes, indeed,' Major Vernon said, also chuckling. 'That does take some getting used to.' He offered Mum and Grandmother Harriet two free tickets to come back and see <u>Johnny Guitar</u> another time (or another film if they preferred), and then he looked at Mum and said, 'I'm looking for another full-time usher, and your coolness under pressure and instinctive ability to handle the public is <u>exactly</u> what I need. Have you got a job at the moment?'

Mum did have a job. In fact, she had two. She was an (early morning) office cleaner at a firm of solicitors near St Paul's Cathedral, and a (late night) cleaner at Bethnal Green Hospital. Mum despised both jobs, and was desperate to find new employment – and she was clearly taken with Major Vernon's squid ink eyes and matinée idol smile (not to mention military nickname) – but Mum (being Mum) said, 'May I think about your offer for a while please?'

'Of course,' Major Vernon said. 'Just let me know by Friday afternoon at the latest.'

Three days later, at five o'clock on Friday afternoon, Mum phoned Major Vernon and accepted his offer.

CHAPTER NINE

I sucked the cock of my Billy Crow. I felt the smooth plum of his helmet slide against the roof of my mouth. I tasted the salt and sweat on him.

Billy was lying alongside me, but in the opposite direction, so he could suck my cock while I sucked his.

My tongue flicked and teased him, as his tongue flicked and teased me.

'I'm . . . going to . . . cum,' I gasped.

'So . . . am . . . I.'

I felt his cock swell in my mouth, and then I became aware of a new taste – harsher, saltier – spilling on my tongue, as my own spunk spurted between Billy's lips.

I felt him licking the spunk from my still-hard cock.

I licked the spunk from *his* still-hard cock.

Billy sat up, turned round, and lay down again to face me.

He kissed me, mixing my spunk with his, and then lay on his back, gazing at the ceiling. 'The crocodiles are watching us,' he said.

The ceiling was now covered with crocodiles, as were all the walls.

I noticed a smaller, simple line drawing of a crocodile in a corner of the ceiling, similar to the one I'd seen on his front door.

'Why does that one look different from all the others?' I asked, pointing.

'Oh! That's my tag,' he said.

'Your . . . *what*?'

'My graffiti name. I put it on everything I create. It's my signature, if you like.'

I looked at him.

A vein pulsed in his neck.

He licked his lips. He sighed. He blinked.

I said, 'I can see crocodiles in your eyes.'

'*Crocodiles in Your Eyes*. That's a good title for a song.'

'You should write it,' I said.

'Perhaps I will,' he said.

I lay in the crook of his arm.

I could stay like this forever.

'They can live for over a hundred years, you know,' Billy said. 'Crocodiles.'

'Can they?'

He nodded. 'You and me . . . we'll live and die, and the crocodiles that are alive now – they will still be here! Safe in their hard skins. We should worship them. They're the only things *worth* worshipping. Sex is the way we do it. Sex beneath a sky of crocodiles. We make each other cum. We taste each other's spunk. Spunk is our Eucharist. This is my Sistine Chapel of Crocodiles.'

My cock was already getting hard again.

'Well . . .' I put his hand on my groin. 'I'm willing to worship here any time.'

Billy laughed. 'I'm in bed with a religious fanatic!'

We kissed.

I heard Liam yelling next door.

'They're back already?!' I said.

Anne had gone to the park again with Liam (without Darryl this time: he was back at work).

'Why d'you say "already"?' Billy asked. 'They've been gone all afternoon.'

'All afternoon!?' I reached for my wristwatch on the floorboards. 'It's six o'clock!'

I've been having sex with Billy for five hours!

'Time flies when you're worshipping crocodiles,' Billy said, smiling and standing up.

'Will you shut the window, please, Billy. I don't want my sister to hear us.'

'We're only talking!'

'*Now* we are, yeah. But ... who knows what might suddenly ... erupt.' I reached out and touched his cock.

Billy smiled. 'I think I need something to drink before I do any more 'erupting'. But to put your mind at rest ...' He headed for the window.

'Put some clothes on first!' I said.

'No one can see me.' He closed the window. 'I'll pop downstairs and get us some Cokes.'

Billy had managed to get an old fridge in the kitchen connected to the electric. When I asked him how he'd done it, he grinned and said, 'Magic!'

'Where're my boots?' Billy was looking round the room.

Walking barefoot on the floorboards risked getting a splinter with every step.

'I can't see them,' I said.

Billy opened the wardrobe door.

'Here they are!' He put them on, their many buckles jingling.

There was only one item of clothing in the wardrobe: a leather jacket. It had been painted green (to resemble crocodile skin) and it was decorated with emerald studs and rhinestones.

'That jacket is ... amazing!' I said.

'My Crocodile Jacket,' Billy said. 'You can try it on if you like.' He went downstairs.

I got up from the mattress and took the jacket off its hanger.

I smelt it: *Billy.*

I put it on.

It felt cool and heavy.

There was a cracked mirror on the back of the wardrobe door. I looked at my reflection.

I ran my hands over the hard surface of the jacket, then across my naked stomach and down to my pubic hair.

'It suits you.' Billy was standing in the doorway, holding two bottles of Coke, and gazing at me.

'I bet it looks better on you.'

Billy gave me a Coke.

'How long did it take you to paint it?' I asked.

'I didn't.'

'Oh?'

'It was a gift.'

'A very *special* gift.'

'That's right.'

'From a . . . very *special* person?'

'No past stuff. Remember?'

'Who were they?'

Billy didn't respond.

'Were they in love with you?'

Billy didn't respond.

'They *must've* been.' I said. 'Who else would give you a jacket like this? Were *you* in love with *them*? How long ago was it? When did you last see them? It is *over*, right?' I grabbed his arm. '*Is* it over? Tell me, Billy . . . *Please!*'

He thought for a moment, gazing at me and sipping Coke. 'Okay. I'll make you a deal. A finger for a question.'

'What d'you mean?'

He got to his knees in front of me. 'Put your Coke down,' he said, placing his own on the floor beside him.

I put my Coke down.

'Spread your legs a little.'

'Like . . . this?'

'Yeah.' He spat over the fingers of his right hand. He looked at the spit, then spat again . . . and again . . .

My cock was pulsing erect, poking up between the open zip of the leather jacket.

Billy put his spit-covered hand between my legs, working it between my buttocks, until he was able to lubricate my anus with his saliva.

He said, 'I'm going to finger fuck you. Okay?'

'. . . Yeah.'

'You *sure*?'

'Yeah, yeah! Do it!'

Billy started pushing a finger inside me.

There was a flare of pain, then a blaze of pleasure.

I moaned and pushed back . . . back . . . feeling the finger slide deeper and deeper inside me.

It hurt, but I wanted the hurt.

When the finger was fully in, Billy said, 'First question.'

It took me moment to catch my breath . . . and my thoughts. Finally I managed, 'Who . . . who gave you . . . the jacket?'

'Someone named Trystan.'

'Was he – ?'

'Wait, wait! A second question requires a second finger.' He started to push another finger into me.

I felt my anus stretching wider.

I moaned louder . . . louder . . .

When the second finger was fully in, Billy said, 'Okay. Second question.'

I was so horny I found it difficult to concentrate.

I said, 'Was this . . . Trystan . . . a friend . . . or a lover?'

'A lover.'

'When were you – ?'

'Wait for the finger!' Billy started pushing a third finger into me.

I cried out, a sharp pain quivering through me.

Billy stopped pushing. 'Relax,' he said.

I relaxed, breathing deep.

Billy started pushing the finger in again. 'Oh, I can feel you opening up for me.'

I want to open for you, Billy.

I want to open for you and only you.

'Okay,' Billy said. 'Ask your question.'

'When . . . when were you seeing Trystan?'

'Last year.'

My cock was throbbing and jerking in front of Billy's face. The helmet was gleaming with pre-cum. Billy's green eyes were staring at me.

I said, 'And it's . . . over?'

'Wait for the finger!'

'I'm cumming!'

Billy grabbed my cock and wrapped his lips around it. I pumped spasm after spasm of spunk into his mouth. I yelled out again and again, dizzy with ecstasy.

When the orgasm was over, Billy got to his feet and pushed me onto the mattress.

I lay flat on my back.

Billy knelt astride me. He opened the leather jacket, revealing my bare chest and stomach. Then he leant forward and slowly, slowly parted his lips.

Spunk and saliva drooled from his mouth and onto my torso.

Billy waited until there was no more cum to come.

He lay beside me, staring up at the crocodiles once again.

I stared at the crocodiles too, as the fireworks in my mind and body gradually fizzled out.

Billy said, 'Well, it's a good job I closed the window. Your orgasm must've measured nine on the Richter scale.'

We laughed.

I said, 'Billy . . . I want to know about you and Trystan. Where did you meet? Where did you live? What did you get up to with him? Why did you – ?'

'That's a fistful of fingers already.'

'I'm being serious.'

'So am I.'

I propped myself up on an elbow and looked at him. 'I don't want to find out about it through . . . the finger method,' I said. And then I smiled. 'Fun though that was.'

Billy said, 'I don't like talking about – '

'Yes, yes, I know. No talking about the past. Only us. Here. Now. But . . . I *have* to know about Trystan, Billy.'

'What does it matter?'

'It matters because . . . he was part of your story. Now I am and . . . Oh, please tell me, Billy! Please! *Please! Please!*'

'Okay, okay, calm down. Let me think about it.' Billy got up and started sorting through the spray cans of paint. 'You'd best go now.'

'Wh-what? Why?'

'I've got work to do.'

'But Trystan – '

'I said I wanted to think about it. I don't . . . I don't want to tell you face to face. I'll think of another way.'

'You promise?'

'Yes! Now go!'

CHAPTER TEN

Anne was in the kitchen when I got back.

'Where have *you* been?' she asked.

'Oh . . . just out,' I said.

'I wish you'd phoned. I was getting worried.'

'Sorry.'

I hadn't yet told Anne about Billy. She'd been out every time I'd gone to see him, and, as yet, hadn't seen me come out of his house, let alone (thanks to Billy closing the window) hear me cum inside it.

'Is Liam in bed?' I asked, sitting at the table with her.

'For the time being. There's some salmon salad in the fridge if you want it.'

'Thanks. I'll have it later.'

'And before you ask, Darryl's not home.'

'*Again?*'

'He's had to go to Glasgow apparently. Urgent delivery.'

'He's away more than he's here.'

'Yeah, I know.'

We sat in silence for a while.

'Darryl was telling me about that model scout,' I said. 'The one who spotted him when he was working on his uncle's stall.'

'Darryl's always going on about that.'

'It's the first time *I've* heard it.'

'But Darryl's always saying, "I could've been a model . . . I could've been a –" '

'Yeah, yeah, I've heard him say *that*. But I thought it

was just a . . . a half-joke sort of thing. I didn't know it was . . . you know. *Real.*'

'Oh, it wasn't "real", Dom.'

'But the model scout – '

'She *wasn't* a model scout. She was a con artist.'

'You met her?'

'I didn't *have* to meet her. Listen. This woman – whoever she was – she said she was going to set up a photo shoot for Darryl. Who had to pay for it? Darryl. She was going to send him to a model agency for an interview. Who had to pay for the privilege of being interviewed? Darryl. She said she'd sort out meetings for him in New York. Who had to pay for the flight, the hotel, all expenses, plus a "scout fee", whatever *that* was? Darryl. The whole thing was a scam. *I* knew it. *Uncle Ernie* knew. *Everyone* knew it.'

'But Darryl said his Uncle Ernie *encouraged* him to – '

'Uncle Ernie was desperate to get shot of him, *that's* why!' Don't get me wrong. Uncle Ernie was a good man. He kept an eye on Darryl while Darryl's mum drank herself to death, and then he all but adopted Darryl when his dad scarpered to God knows where.'

'So why did Uncle Ernie want to – ?'

'Because dear ol' Uncle Ernie had fallen in love with the man who owned the jewellers opposite his stall, and the two of them had decided to sell up and retire to a villa in Spain. The *last* thing Uncle Ernie wanted was ever-needy Darryl following them out there. Which is why, of course, he *so* wanted to believe that Darryl could be a model in New York, and – when that failed – gave Darryl and me the down payment on this house. It was a lovely gift. Of course it was. But it was still a gift that benefited Uncle Ernie every bit as much as it benefited me and Darryl.'

'MUM!' Liam cried from the nursery.

'Duty calls.' Anne got up and went into the house.

I was standing up to go inside as well when I heard Billy's back door open.

Candlelight flickered through the foliage.

He's in his garden!

'Billy?' I said, softly.

He started walking down the garden.

I followed, watching out for glimpses of fire.

'Billy?'

Candlelight . . . darkness . . . candlelight . . .

He stopped by the hole in the fence, where I'd taken the gold Cadillac from his hand two days before.

I peered through it.

'Billy?'

'Shhh.' He put something in the hole, nestling it in the vines and roses.

It was an envelope.

A letter?

I took it from the foliage.

On the front of the envelope was written:

Dom

'Billy? Have you written to me about – ?'

'Shhh.'

Billy started to walk back towards his house.

'It's about you and Trystan, isn't it?' I asked, keeping parallel with his candlelight

Billy didn't answer. He just opened the back door and went inside.

This is the story of how Mum got a big film premiere to happen at the Rex cinema.

Within a year of starting work at the Rex Mum had been promoted to chief usher, and everyone who worked there – including Major Vernon – agreed that she could run the place single-handed should the occasion ever arise. In many ways, ushering at the Rex was the perfect job for Mum: she loved the movies, the pale avocado uniform (with gold braid trimmings) suited her to a T, and she'd been born with the unfailing knack of being totally pleasant to total strangers (it was friends and family Mum had trouble with).

Mum did all the overtime she could because, yes, she loved the job, but more so because it took her mind off Grandmother Harriet, whose health was getting worse and worse. For a while, Mum, on her afternoons off, brought Grandmother Harriet to the Rex in a wheelchair, which meant Grandmother Harriet had to sit in the stalls, (to be close to the toilets, which were on the ground floor), but following a very distressing incident during the opening credits of <u>East of Eden</u>, their trips to the cinema stopped altogether.

Most of the regular patrons had got to know Mum by her first name, and Mum was in the habit of asking them for their opinions about what films they wanted to see, and ways the Rex could be improved. One of the patrons said, 'Why don't you have a premiere of a big film so that lots of movie stars will come and we can get their autographs.'

Mum said, 'Oh, that's a charming idea, but it simply won't be possible, I'm afraid. Film premieres only happen in big cinemas in the West End of London, not small East End cinemas like this.'

But, the next day, on her way to visit Grandmother Harriet, who was 'under observation' in London Hospital, Mum saw a film crew standing outside the hospital's main entrance.

A youth was stopping pedestrians.

'What're you filming?' Mum asked him.

'The new Dirk Bogarde film, miss,' he said.

Dirk Bogarde was a famous matinée idol at the time (very handsome and, according to Mum, 'so well spoken').

'What's the film called?' Mum asked.

'It's another of Mr Bogarde's "Doctor" comedies, miss. It's called Doctor in the Slums.'

'"The slums"? Do you mean . . . around here?'

'That's right, miss.' He noticed the startled sorrow on Mum's face, so quickly added, 'The East End's not a slum to people like us, of course. But to a gentleman like Mr Bogarde it is. You understand me, don't you, miss?'

Mum did understand him (she understood him only too well), which is why she made out she hadn't heard, and said, 'I work at a local cinema. The Rex. It would be the perfect place to premiere Mr Bogarde's film. Who do I talk to about that?'

'Oh . . . well . . . everyone's a bit busy at the moment, miss. I tell you what, give me your name and the phone number of the cinema and I'll get the producer to give you a call.'

Mum wrote it on the back of a bus ticket she found in her bag.

'Major Vernon is the manager of the cinema,' she said. 'The producer should ask to speak to him.'

'I'm sure he will, miss – Move along now!'

Mum went into the hospital and made her way to her mother's ward. A nurse stopped her just as she was approaching Grandmother Harriet's bed.

'Your mother's in a very melancholy mood today,' the nurse said. 'Try to cheer her up.'

'I always do,' Mum said. She went to her mother's bedside. 'I've got some great news! I've just arranged a big premiere at the Rex.'

When the Prince was born
the Queen said, 'My child is the most
beautiful thing in the whole universe.
And everyone in the Castle agreed.
(Of course they did).

But there was a problem.
When the Prince had taken
his first breath
he started to cry.
And the crying didn't stop.
It went on and on and on and on.
For hours...days...weeks...

Doctors and wise men were summoned
from every corner of the land.

They all offered advice.
Everything was tried.
Nothing worked.

Eventually,
the Queen went to a Wizard
and said, 'Do something to make
the Prince stop crying.'

This Wizard said, 'Give the Prince this.'
And he put a large egg
in the Queen's hands.

'What's inside it?' the Queen asked.
The Wizard replied, 'So long as
it makes Prince stop crying,
what does it matter?'

When the Queen got back to the Castle
she put the egg beside the Prince.
The Prince looked at the egg.
The Prince touched the egg.
And the Prince stopped crying.

Everyone in the Castle
was thrilled to have a
good night's sleep at last,
but everyone was asking
the same question
the Queen had asked:
'What's in the egg?'

PART TWO

CHAPTER ELEVEN

Dear Dom,

I guess you're wondering why I'm writing to you about Trystan instead of simply telling you.

I am.

I'm doing it because, if I told you the story to your face, I would notice your reactions, and I'd be tempted to change the story in order to please you. Just like any performer adapts what they're doing to satisfy their audience. Expand what the audience wants, diminish what it doesn't want. But I don't want to do that. I want to tell you the truth.

Are you ready?

Yes!

One day I went to have my photo taken in a photo booth machine. I didn't need the photo for a passport or anything like that. I needed it because I didn't have a camera and it was my eighteenth birthday, and I wanted to have a record of how I looked on that very special day.

That's what I did!

I should tell you straightaway that, on my eighteenth

birthday, I looked <u>very</u> different from the way you see me now. I didn't have a Mohican haircut. I didn't have green hair. I wasn't wearing the Crocodile Jacket. Nor I did have any tattoos. I looked pretty much like any other teenager.

I can't imagine you looking like 'any other teenager', Billy.

Except, perhaps, that all my clothes were black: black jeans, black T-shirt, black lace-up shoes.

All my clothes are black too! You must've noticed that, Billy.

People were always saying to me, 'Whose funeral are you going to?'

That's what Mum says to me!

The photo booth I went to was at the local tube station. I was just about to go in when someone who worked there came up to me and said, 'Sorry. It's not working.' He put an 'OUT OF ORDER' sign on the machine, saying, 'A young gentleman had his photo taken a little while ago and the photos never came out. The machine should be fixed by tomorrow.' But, of course, tomorrow would be too late. I needed the photo today. My birthday.

I stood there, trying to think of where else I could try. And that's when the photo booth started to make clunking noises. The next second, a strip of four photographs fell into the receptacle tray. It must be the photos of the 'young gentleman' who'd used the machine before me.

I picked the photos up.

They were of someone, about my age, with a black quiff and wearing a white T-shirt and a red denim jacket. He was looking straight into the camera and smiling with such cocksure confidence that it oozed from the photo like ectoplasm.

Ectoplasm!?

I could feel the spirit of him all around me. It made me feel safe and less lonely. I took the photographs home with me.

Really?!

That night, I lay in bed and gazed at the photographs. I imaged what it would be like to meet the person with the black quiff and cocksure smile. I imagined how we'd look walking along the street together, holding hands. I imagined the feel of his skin: the warmth of it, the gentle yet secure grip. I imagined the way he'd gaze into my eyes and say, 'You are my only love.'

You what!?

Over the next week I imagined more and more about him. He liked music. He had a large record collection. His favourite singer was Elvis Presley. He was friendly, and everyone liked him. He had a job at . . . where? A cinema! That's it. He was an usher!

Like Mum used to be! There's a lot of coincidences in this letter, Billy.

He would come home from work, go to his room and play records all evening. And when I say 'his room', I didn't mean his bedroom at his parents' place. Oh. no. He lived . . . where? . . . In a bedsit! Yes! I could see it all! The bedsit had one window. The window had a Venetian blind. It was illuminated by neon — bright green neon! — coming from outside. There was a single bed, a wardrobe (with a cracked mirror), a damp patch on the ceiling.

The only thing I couldn't make up my mind about him was . . . his name. Nothing felt right. So, until one revealed itself, I simply referred to him as My Only Love — Oh, I know you're thinking, Dom. This is all a bit strange.

More than a bit.

Well, I don't care. Yes, he was a fantasy. But I loved him. Okay?

If you say so.

And then, one day, I went to the zoo.

The zoo!?

I'd been there a few times to sketch the animals. I was especially fond of the crocodiles (the zoo had quite a famous Crocodile House). I was standing in front of the protective glass sketching the crocodiles when someone stood beside me.

My eyes shifted focus from the crocodiles to the person's reflection.

I saw a black quiff, a white T-shirt, and a red denim jacket.

It's the person in the photographs!

I heard him say, 'They're beautiful, aren't they. The crocodiles.'

'Yeah,' I said, turning to face him. 'I love to draw them.'

'I'm glad to hear you say that.' He gave me that cocksure grin of his.

It was the person in the photographs. You've probably already guessed that.

Yep.

'Let me see your drawing,' he said.

'It's not very good.'

'Show me! <u>Please!</u>'

I showed him.

He said, 'I like it.'

'Really?'

'Yes. Really.' He gazed at me. 'Goodness, your eyes are so green. They're perfect. I mean perfectly beautiful.'

'Thank you.'

'What's your name?'

'Billy,' I said.

'Do you fancy getting a Coke or something, Billy?'

'Yeah!' I said, perhaps a little too eagerly.

We went to the zoo's café. We talked all afternoon. We were still talking when the zoo started to close. We walked out of the zoo together.

He told me things about himself and — oh, this is the most

remarkable thing! — nearly everything I had imagined about My Only Love was correct: he _did_ live in a bedsit, he _did_ like music, and he _did_ work as an usher in a cinema!

I got his favourite singer wrong, though: it was Dusty Springfield, not Elvis Presley.

And . . . oh, yes! My Only Love told me his name.

It was Trystan.

Trystan Finch.

Yours Truly.
Billy
XXX

CHAPTER TWELVE

'Dom! . . . DOM!'

'Eh? . . . Wh-what?'

'MUM'S ON THE PHONE!'

'OKAY!' I struggled out of bed.

I'd been reading (and re-reading) Billy's letter for most of the night, had finally dropped off to sleep just as the sun was rising and –

'DOM! HURRY!'

'I'M COMING!'

I went downstairs.

Anne handed me the phone, asking, 'Do you want some breakfast?'

'Just some toast. Thanks . . . Hello, Mum.'

Anne went to the kitchen as –

'What're you doing still in bed?' Mum asked. 'I hope you weren't out on the town last night.'

'When have you *ever* known me to do that?'

'I never knew your *sister* do to that . . . until that's *all* she did.'

'Mum, Anne has *never* – '

'Why haven't you phoned me?'

'Sorry, Mum. I've . . . I've been busy.'

'Doing what?'

'Working.'

'*What* work?'

'My writing and – '

'Oh, *that's* not work. You need to get a summer job.

You can't expect your sister to keep you. She's barely got enough money to look after herself. Me and your dad would have kept you. That's what parents *do* for their children. But your sister – Let *me* do that, Lionel!'

'What's happening?'

'Your Dad's trying to put the Hoover away. It weighs a tonne – Lionel! You'll give yourself another heart attack! I'll do it . . . Okay, okay. I'll bring you some lemonade in a moment. Have a rest.' She sighed. 'He's gone to the balcony.'

'Is he okay?'

'He's fine.'

'Why isn't he at work, then?'

'We've got a hospital appointment at two o'clock. Just a regular check-up. Nothing to worry about. I've told Anne we'll pop round after for a visit.'

'Pop round . . . *here*?'

'Don't sound so surprised.'

'I . . . I'm not. I'm happy. That's great.'

'We'll be there by four.'

'Okay.'

'You'll *be* there?'

'Of course I will. And Mum . . . can you bring some stuff from my room?'

'Oh, we haven't got time to pack everything and put it in the car and – '

'Just the books left on the shelves. And the folders by the desk. It should all fit into a few boxes.'

'I don't think we've *got* any boxes.'

'Carrier bags, then. Anything. *Please*, Mum.'

'I'll talk to your dad about it. See you later. Bye.'

'Bye.' I put the phone down and went to the kitchen. 'We're getting a royal visit, then,' I said to Anne.

'So it appears.' She put a cup of tea and a plate of toast

in front of me. 'I'll give the place a quick tidy before they arrive.' She sat down, sighing. 'At least Liam's in a more manageable mood today.'

I could see him in the garden playing with his cars. Which, of course, reminded me of the gold Cadillac Billy had given me.

I need to speak to Billy about his letter!

I finished breakfast as quickly as I could and then rushed upstairs to get washed and dressed.

When I came back down Anne was putting Liam in his pushchair.

She said, 'I'm off to the supermarket to get some stuff for this afternoon. Salmon and cucumber. For sandwiches. And I'll get us a cake. Perhaps one of those frozen ones with ice cream inside. Do you think Mum would like that?'

'You can give it a try.'

'Perhaps I'll stick with a Bakewell tart. At least we know she actually *eats* that – Will you wash up the breakfast things while I'm gone?'

'Yeah, yeah, sure.'

'And give the garden a tidy. Liam dropped a choc ice on the patio.'

'Okay.'

'I'll see you later, then.'

'Yeah.'

'I *mean* it, Dom. Do *not* disappear and leave me to cope with Mum alone.'

'I won't, I won't. Promise.'

'Okay . . . Bye.'

'Bye.'

I started to wash up the breakfast things but, after a couple of minutes, my need to talk to Billy got the better of me.

I rushed next door.

I knocked.

No answer.

I looked through the letter box.

I could see Billy's shadow on the stairs.

Why's he ignoring me?

I knocked again.

'Billy!' I called.

Still no answer.

I knocked louder, more frantically.

'I know you're in there, Billy! Open the door! Open the door! Open the –'

The door swung open.

'I'm busy, Dom!' Billy said.

He was holding a can of spray paint. Green and gold were speckled over his naked torso.

'I need to talk to you. *Please.*' I pushed past him and into the house.

'What're you in such a state about?'

'Your letter –'

'No! I don't want to talk about anything in the –'

'I took a photograph of myself too!'

'Eh? What?'

'On my eighteenth birthday. I took a photograph of myself. Just like you did.'

'. . . Okay. So?'

'So don't you think that's a coincidence?'

'Lots of people take photos of themselves on –'

'I'm sure they don't!'

'Well, I'm sure they do!'

'And why didn't you tell me about wearing black?'

'*What?*'

'You said you used to wear black.'

'I did.'

'*I* wear black. All the time. As you can see? I'm known for it.'

'You're *"known"* for it?!'

'My mum's always saying, "Whose funeral you going to?" Just like people used to say to you. Another coincidence!'

'Dom, Dom, calm down.'

'There's more! Mum used to be an usher. At a cinema. Just like Trystan.'

'I . . . I don't know where you're going with this.'

'*All* these coincidences! In *one* letter!'

'Listen, Dom. You're reading too much into . . . all this. Coincidences . . . just happen. Life's full of them. You need to stop reading books and live a bit more.'

'Says the person who's . . . what? A whole year older than me?'

'And I've lived a million lifetimes in that year!'

'Oh, what a *very* Billy Crow thing to say.'

'What's *that* supposed to mean?'

'It means you can be such a pretentious wanker sometimes.'

'Only "sometimes"?' He grinned. 'I'll have to work harder at it then, won't I?' The grin turned to a smile. 'Honestly, Dom. I don't know why you're getting yourself so worked up about this.'

'I'm getting "so worked up" because . . . I want to talk to you and you're . . . you're pushing me away.'

'I'm *not* doing that, Dom.'

'You are! Sometimes I think you're just playing games with me.'

'No. This is *not* a game.'

'Well, that's what it feels like!'

'That's *your* problem, not *mine*. Now, enough of this! I've got a lot of work to do!' He pointed at the upper

hallway. Crocodiles were on the wall outside the bathroom and starting to work their way down the stairs.
'My crocodiles are calling – pretentious enough for you?
– and I've got no time for all your childish – '

'I'm not being child – '

'You are! You wanted to know about Trystan and I am
telling you.'

'You . . . you "*are telling*" me?'

'Yes.'

'Present continuous tense?'

'Don't show off.'

'But it means you'll *continue* to tell me.'

'Correct.'

'When?'

'Soon.'

'*How* soon?'

'As soon as the crocodiles fill the hallway.'

'When will that be?'

'Never. If you stop me painting them. Now go away
and – '

'I'll come back this evening and – '

'No. *I'll* contact *you*.'

'But when? . . . *When*, Billy?'

'I can't tell you that!' His green eyes glinted. 'You're
beginning to piss me off now, Dom.'

I've pushed it too far!

I said, 'Okay, okay. I'm going.'

I stepped out of the house.

He shut the door behind me.

*I can't go back next door. I'll just sit in my room and think
about Billy and Trystan in that bedsit together.*

I started walking down the street as –

*Did Billy kiss Trystan's neck like he kissed mine? – No, no!
Stop thinking about it!*

I walked and walked and walked.

Did Billy suck Trystan like he sucked me?

Did Trystan spunk in Billy's mouth and – Stop!

I was on Bethnal Green Road now. Quite a distance from where I'd started.

How long have I been walking?

I looked at my wristwatch.

Two hours!

I was approaching the Rex.

It couldn't be this cinema where Trystan worked. Or, per-haps, still works. Not the same cinema where Mum used to be an usher. That would be too much of a coincidence.

It can't be this cinema.

It can't be.

It can't.

But it might.

I went into the Rex.

CHAPTER THIRTEEN

The entrance foyer still looked impressive, with its scarlet carpet and yucca plants, but most of the gilt curlicue trimmings had been removed altogether, when – during some serious renovation a few years ago – the venue officially became the Rex Multiplex (it now has five small screens instead of one big one).

I looked around: there was no one anywhere.

I called, 'Hello?'

No response.

'HELLO?'

Someone yelled, 'I WON'T KEEP YOU A MOMENT!'

I paced around, looking at the posters for 'Forthcoming Attractions': *Grease 2, Conan the Barbarian, Death Wish II, Porky's, E.T.* –

'Hello. Sorry.' The person who'd called had come out of a doorway beneath the stairs. He was about my age, with platinum blond hair (sharply cut, with a swept-back fringe), and the broad-shouldered, sleek physique of a swimmer. He was wearing white chinos, a Ben Sherman shirt, and glasses (which had slid down his nose a little). He was clutching a mop and bucket. 'We've had a major freezer meltdown in the basement.' He put the bucket and mop down. 'And I'm here all alone. Usher-wise, that is. The others have all called in sick. But I suspect they've gone to the seaside. I can't blame them. Who'd want to be stuck in here when the weather's like this? There's hardly anyone to sell tickets to anyway. Okay. Time to be professional.' He wiped his hands on his shirt, and pushed his glasses back to the top of his nose. 'Welcome to the legendary Rex Multiplex, sir. The most famous cinema in the East End of London. How can I help you?'

'I . . . I only want to ask . . . does somebody called Trystan work here?'

'Not that I know of.'

'Well . . . *did* a Trystan work here . . . in the last year or so?'

'I couldn't answer that. I'm new here. Summer job.'

'Well . . . would the manager know?'

'I guess so, yeah.'

'Is he here? Or is it a she now?'

'No, no, it's a he. Mr Ellroy . . . You're not a private detective, are you?'

'No, I am *not!*'

'That was meant as a joke.'

'Oh. Sorry.'

'Tell me, has this Trystan got a second name?'

'Finch.'

'Trystan Finch. Okay. Won't keep you a moment.' He dashed up the stairs, two at a time.

I really like his white chinos.

A couple of minutes later he was two-at-a-timing back down.

He must have great leg muscles.

'The manager has no recollection of a Trystan Finch working here,' he said. 'Certainly not in the last two and a half years he's been manager.'

'Oh . . . okay. Thanks for checking.'

'Anything else I can help you with?'

'Well . . . I could do with an ice cream but –'

'Freezer meltdown.'

'Exactly.'

'We do films as well as ice creams. And we've got plenty of those. The next one starts in . . . oh, thirty minutes. You could see that if you like.'

He's got a lovely smile.

'What is it?'

'*Peter Pan.*'

'I've never seen it.'

'It's part of our *Walt Disney Summer Season.* Manager's idea. New film every week. Last week was *The Sword in the Stone.*'

'Oh, I've seen *that!*'

'It's not bad. *Peter Pan*'s better. I can sneak you in if you want to check it out. Of course, it would mean hanging around for half an hour. But I thought . . . we could . . . chat and . . . get to know each other a bit. If you want to. Perhaps you *don't* want to. In which case, forget I said anything.'

That smile!

'I *do* want to,' I said.

'Really?'

'Really.'

'Well, that's . . . that's great! I can get you something to drink from the staffroom fridge. *That's* still working, thank goodness. I can offer you a Coke . . . or a Coke.'

'I think I'll have a Coke, please.' I held out my hand. 'I'm Dominic. Dom.'

'Sebastian. Seb.'

We shook hands.

'I'll get you a Coke, Dom.'

A few minutes later we sitting on a couple of chairs outside the entrance to Screen Number One (the largest of the five screens). There was a table nearby with a book on it: *The Life & Tragic Death of King Edward II.*

'Is that yours?' I asked.

'Afraid so.'

'Heavy reading.'

'I'm going to university in September.'

'So am I. Well, to college.'

'Where?'

'St Martin's School of Art.'

'Didn't the Sex Pistols do their first gig there?'

'That's right. When I went for the interview one of the students showed me some graffiti. It was done by Johnny Rotten himself.'

'Very cool.'

'Yeah.'

The Coke's making his lips wet.

I asked, 'And where're *you* going to study, Seb?'

'Queen Mary University.'

'Down by Mile End?'

'That's right. I can walk there in twenty minutes from where I live.'

'And you're going to study history?' I indicated the book on the table.

'*Very* well deduced, my dear Holmes.'

'Elementary, my dear Watson.'

He pushed his glasses back up his nose.

He looks so cute when he does that.

I asked, 'And *where* do you live that's a twenty minute walk away from – ?'

'Oasis Estate. Bottom of Cambridge Heath Road.'

'My mum and dad were going to move there! When they first got married. But they ended up in Bradley Estate.'

'I know where you mean. Lots of graffiti.'

'Yeah. My mum hates it.'

'Why doesn't she move?'

'Oh, I don't know. It's like . . . people just get sort of . . . stuck. You know? Mum doesn't like living there . . . but it's too much effort to get out.'

'Do *you* want to get out?'

'I already have. This week.'

'Well done! Where are you now?'

'Bow.'

'That's just a short bus ride from me.'

'You can pop round for a visit.'

'I'd like that.'

I want to kiss him.

He asked, 'Do you live by yourself?'

'No. With my older sister.'

'I live with my older brother!'

'Really?'

'Yeah.'

I sipped some Coke.

He sipped some Coke.

I asked, 'Where do your parents live, Seb?'

He hesitated a moment. And then took a deep breath and said, 'Okay. I'm about to hit you with a heavy bit of information. Apologies in advance. You ready?'

'. . . Okay.'

'I haven't got any parents. Dad left before I was born. No one knew where he went. No one cared. And mum . . . she died last year.'

'Oh, I . . . I'm sorry.'

'It's okay. Well, it's not okay, but . . .' He took a gulp of Coke. 'Have you always been interested in art?'

'Oh, yeah. I didn't have many friends when I was a kid. So I sort of created my own. I drew pictures of them. I wrote stories about them. I wasn't sure if I should go on to study English literature or art. But, in the end, I decided on art. I thought I can always read books, but I need to go somewhere to learn how to do oil painting and photography and all the other things I want to do and . . . oh, listen to me. Jabbering on like this. Sorry. I must be boring you.'

'No!' He leant forward, eyes eager. 'I want to know *everything* about you.'

I reached out and touched his hand. 'I want to know everything about you too,' I said.

His skin's so smooth!

'And I'll tell you,' Seb said. 'But it'll have to wait till after *Peter Pan*. It's just about to start. It's in Screen 3. Over there. You go on in. No need for a ticket. I've got some work to do, but I'll pop in and sit with you whenever I can. I should warn you though. The air conditioning in this place is useless.'

'*Famously* useless.'

'Exactly. So it'll be as hot and humid as the Colombian jungle in there. Not that I've ever been to the Colombian jungle. But you know what I mean.'

That smile again!

I said. 'I'll be in the front row.'

'I like the front row too.'

I went into the auditorium. It was every bit as hot and humid as Seb had warned me.

I sat in the middle of the front row.

I wish Seb was sitting beside me.

I settled back to watch the film.

I enjoyed it. But my thoughts of Seb kept getting in the way.

He's so easy to talk to. I bet lots of people fancy him. How many has he kissed? I bet he's kissed lots.

'This is my favourite bit.' Seb slipped into the seat beside me. 'Watch!'

On the screen Peter is sprinkling pixie dust on Wendy

and her siblings. They all fly through the open window, soaring over London, past Big Ben and the Tower of London, then higher and further, heading for the second star to the right and –

Seb squeezed my hand!

I squeezed his hand back. And we stayed like that, fingers stroking fingers, till Seb whispered, 'Work to do,' and dashed out of the auditorium.

When the cartoon crocodile appeared in the film – all grinning and gurning, and playing it for laughs – I did wonder what Billy would have thought. But not for long. Because all I really wanted to think about was Seb. Seb. Seb. Seb. Seb. Seb. Seb. Seb. Seb. Seb. Seb. Seb. Seb. Seb. Seb. Seb. Seb. Seb. Seb. Seb. Seb. Seb. Seb. Seb. Seb. Seb. Seb. Seb. Seb. Seb. Seb. Seb. Seb. Seb. Seb. Seb. Seb. Seb. Seb. Seb. Seb. Seb. Seb. Seb. Seb. Seb. Seb. Seb. Seb. Seb. Seb –

He popped back just as the end credits started to roll.

We left the auditorium together.

Seb said all the ushers for the next shift had turned up, so he was free to leave now.

Outside, the sunlight made me squint.

'Do you fancy a bite to eat, Dom?'

'Yeah,' I said. 'I'm starving.'

We walked to the McDonald's. We both ordered a cheeseburger with medium fries, and a strawberry milkshake. We sat by the window to eat.

I told him about Mum once working at the Rex, and how she'd managed to get *Doctor in the Slums* to premiere there.

I said, 'There was a photograph of her in the *East London Chronicle*. All the staff outside the cinema holding –'

'Champagne glasses! I've seen it!'

'Really?'

'It's in the manager's office. What one's your mum?'

'Third from the left.'

'The glamorous one!'

Mum glamorous? The thought had never occurred to me before. But, yes, I suppose she was. Still is.

The sun was beginning to set by the time we left McDonald's.

I said I'd walk Seb home.

We walked slowly.

We walked and talked and it felt wonderful.

And then, for a while, we walked and didn't talk and that felt wonderful too.

When we got to Seb's estate the sky was bright red.

'What a brilliant sunset.' Seb said.

'I want to kiss you,' I said.

'That's the most thrilling non sequitur I've ever heard.'

'I've got another one. Is your brother at home?'

'He shouldn't be, no.'

'So . . . can I kiss you . . . in your room?' I pulled him to me. 'Please say yes.'

'I will say yes . . . but not now.'

'Oh?'

'If you come back to my room and we kiss . . . well, one kiss will lead to another kiss, and then another kiss, and before we know it we'll be – '

'Heading for the second star to the right and – '

'Exactly. And I *do* want that.'

'Oh, so do I.'

'Oh, I can *see* you do. But can we . . . can take things a little more slowly please. I need a bit more . . . a bit more pixie dust before I feel confident with my flying.'

'Have you . . . flown before?' I asked.

'Not . . . really.'

' "Not really"?'

'Okay. No. I haven't.'

'Not with anyone?'

'That's right. I can tell *you've* been an expert flyer for *quite* a while.'

'That's not true,' I said.

'Well, you're acting like it,' Seb said.

'Well, to be honest, so are you.'

'I know. I'm surprising myself. *Scaring* myself . . . How many have you actually . . . flown with before? If you don't mind me asking.'

'One.'

'*Just* one?'

'Yes.'

'When?'

'. . . Recently.'

'And is it over?'

'. . . I have no intention of ever flying with him again. I promise. And if we continue with this flying metaphor any longer I will spontaneously combust.'

We laughed.

Seb said, 'I think we should have an official "first date".'

'Good idea. When?'

'Tomorrow?'

'Perfect!'

'Why don't you come round for me? Here. I finish a bit earlier on Saturdays. I should be home by four.'

'What's your flat number?'

'32. Top floor.'

'I'll be there.'

I went to kiss him on the lips, but he turned slightly so I caught his cheek.

'More pixie dust before the lips,' Seb said

'*More Pixie Dust Before the Lips,*' I said. 'Good title for a song,' I said.

'It's more a line of poetry, I think.'

'... You're right.'

'And not a very good one.'

I laughed. 'Right again.'

CHAPTER FOURTEEN

By the time I got home (I decided to walk, not catch a bus) the bright red sunset had gone, and the sky was brilliant with stars.

I couldn't see any candlelight flickering through the glass in Billy's front door.

Has he finished painting the hallway?

It was a relief – and a bit of a shock – to realize I didn't really care if he had or hadn't. My mind was too full of Seb.

I went to Anne's house and let myself in.

I stumbled over something in the hall.

Carrier bags full of –

My paperbacks.

I looked in another bag.

My notebooks! Oh, no! Mum and Dad's visit!

'The prodigal brother returns!' I heard Anne call from the living room.

I went to her.

The main light was out. The television was on, but the sound was down. A James Bond film – *Diamonds Are Forever* – was in its final reel shootout: bullets, bombs, and bikinis.

Anne was sitting on the sofa, Liam curled up beside her, his head on her lap, fast asleep.

'Anne, I'm so, *so* sorry,' I said.

Anne continued gazing at the television screen. 'I haven't asked you to do anything since you moved in here,' she said, explosions in her eyes. 'Well, some weeding of the garden. But apart from that . . . nothing. Except for today.' Her voice was low and measured. 'Today I asked you to tidy the house and clean the choc ice up in the garden, and – the thing you *promised* me you'd do – be here for Mum and Dad's visit.'

'I . . . I just went out to . . . to do some sketching and – '

'Where are they, then?'

'Eh?'

'These bloody sketches you just had to go out and do. Show them to me. *Show me!*'

'I . . . I . . .'

'Why are you lying to me, Dom?'

'I'm not.'

'Stop it! You're treating me *exactly* like you treat Mum. I thought you came here because you wanted to end all the lies and – '

'I'm *not* lying!'

'You *are*! It's just what you do. You lie. You keep secrets. No one ever knows what you're up to. I've barely seen you since you've been here. So much for me thinking you'd be a bit of company.'

'Okay, okay. I'll tell you what happened!'

Anne stared at me, waiting.

'I only said I was sketching because I didn't want to say anything about what *really* happened until . . . until I was totally sure . . . something really *was* happening.'

'I have *no* idea what you're talking about.'

'Okay.' Deep breath. 'I think I've . . . met someone.'

'You mean "met someone" as in . . . "*met someone*"?'

'Yes.'

Anne's eyes grew wide. 'More! I want *more!*'

'Well . . . I met him this afternoon.'

'Where?'

'The Rex.'

'You didn't go to see a film on a day like this *surely*!?
You know what the Rex's air conditioning is like.'

'No, no. I didn't see a film. I was just passing the
cinema and . . . well, he works there and I saw him and
. . . we just . . . started talking and . . . you know.'

'No.' Her eyes twinkled. '*Tell* me.'

'We . . . we took off like a rocket! POW!'

'Don't wake Liam.'

'Sorry. He wants to see me again.'

'Name? *Name?*'

'Sebastian. Seb. We've got a date tomorrow.'

'A date!'

'My first.'

'I'm excited.'

'Not as much as me,' I said. 'He's all I can think of,
Anne. *That's* why I forgot about . . . everything else.'

'Well . . . you hadn't met this Seb when you left the
house without cleaning the garden but . . . well, I'll forgive you that little plot hole if the rest is true.'

'It is. Cross my heart.'

Liam stirred in his sleep.

Anne smoothed his hair.

'How *were* Mum and Dad?' I asked.

'Well, Mum was livid you weren't here, of course.'

'Of course.'

'Especially after she'd gone to the "endless amount of
trouble" packing the stuff you wanted from your room.
But, apart from that, it was . . . oh, it was okay, I suppose.'

'Dad's hospital appointment? How did that go?'

'Fine. Apparently. And Dad says he's never felt better.
I want him to see more of Liam. Liam has to know his
granddad more. He needs those memories. Just in case.
You know?'

'Yeah.'

'Perhaps it's time to ... heal things. For Liam and Dad's sake.'

'Well, Mum seems to be making a bit of an effort. Coming round to visit.'

'Yeah, she *is* making an effort. And I'm *glad* she's doing it. But ... what happened between me and her ... it's not going to be easy to ... to forgive. You know?'

'I'm sure the more you see each other ... and the more Mum sees Liam ... the easier it will be for Mum to –'

'I'm not talking about *Mum* forgiving *me*!' Anne said. 'I'm talking about *me* forgiving *her*.'

'I ... well, yes. I know that.'

'No! You don't! You still think I fell head over heels in love with Darryl, and it was *him* who persuaded me to stop going to church with Mum, and, as a result of losing that vital "moral guidance", I got pregnant and –'

'Stop it, Anne! Where's all this come from? I don't give a toss about the church. You *know* that! It was *me* who took the piss out of you for going in the *first* bloody place!'

Anne took a few deep breaths. 'I know, I know. I'm ... I'm sorry. Mum being here all afternoon has made me a bit ... prickly.'

Liam stirred in his sleep.

Anne stroked his hair, soothing him, and, by so doing, soothed herself.

'Anyway,' Anne said, 'I stopped going to church *weeks* before I met Darryl.'

'Did you? I ... I don't remember.'

'Of course you don't. All anyone remembers is Mum's version about what happened. And Mum, as we both know, is one hell of a storyteller.'

I waited.

Anne continued stroking Liam's hair. 'It was after choir practice one evening. I went to close the windows at the back of the church like I always did. I went into Father Leonard's office. The window there is a high one. You need to stand on a chair to do it. As I got off the chair I lost my balance. I knocked Father Leonard's briefcase off his desk. I went to pick it up. Some magazines had fallen out. With naked women on the covers.'

'. . . Oh,' I said.

Anne looked at me. 'Now, I'm no prude, Dom. You know that. Men can wank themselves silly for all I care. But these magazines . . . they belonged to a man who preached . . . well, you know the sort of stuff he spouted. And yet here he was – this self-righteous pillar of the community – with a briefcase full of . . .' She shook her head. 'It was the sheer bloody hypocrisy of it that sickened me. That's all. And, before you ask, no, I didn't say anything to Father Leonard. I just put everything back in place, walked out of the office, and said, 'See you tomorrow, Father.' But I knew I'd never go back.'

'Why didn't you tell *me*?'

'Dom, you were only . . . how old? Fourteen? And why should I mention it anyway? It wasn't as if it made me "lose my faith" or anything. I didn't have any faith *to* lose. I only ever went to church to keep Mum company. You know that.'

'And the social life. You *did* enjoy that.'

'True. The people there were lovely. And I adored organizing the Nativity. Even *you* helped with that.'

'Yeah, yeah, it was fun.'

'Fun . . . but no faith.'

'And all the better for it.'

'And what about Mum? I'm guessing you never told her.'

'On the way home that night – after I'd found the magazines – I did *intend* to tell her – but ... well, when I got back ... oh, she and Dad were laughing about something, and they were both in such a good mood, I decided to tell her the next day. But the next day ... I couldn't seem to find the right moment. And it kept going on like that.' Anne looked at me. 'What *is* the right time to tell your mum the priest she idolizes has a briefcase full of porn?' She paused for a moment, and then said, 'I did tell Zoë. That was before she'd turned into the bitch from hell, of course.'

Zoë – Anne's best friend (the one who could type sixty words a minute) – had, apparently, fancied Darryl from the moment they all met (on that hot Sunday in Southend). Zoë became very jealous of Anne's relationship with Darryl. So jealous in fact that, a few days before Anne and Darryl were due to get married (at the Hackney Town Hall registry office), Zoë stopped speaking to Anne altogether.

Anne's deep affection for Zoë – they'd known each other since nursery school! – turned to utter contempt.

I didn't want Anne to get stuck in her ranting groove about Zoë (once in, it was difficult to get her out), so I asked, 'Did you tell Darryl about the magazines?'

Anne shook her head. 'If I told him there'd always be the worry he'd blurt something out to Mum. And ... well, I'd pretty much decided *not* to tell her. What was the point? I was off having fun with Darryl. Father bloody Leonard didn't matter anymore. And when I thought about the magazines – if I did at all – I just laughed. It all seemed like a bit of a bad taste joke now. A scene from a *Carry On* film or something. The priest with dirty magazines. You know? And I would have kept on thinking that ... were it not for

. . . for what Mum said when I told her I was pregnant.'

I waited.

Anne stopped stroking Liam's hair. ' "You've let me down," Mum said. "You've let your family down. And, worst of all, you've let Father Leonard down." And *that's* when I told her. About the magazines. And d'you know what she did? She called me a liar. She said, "You're making it all up to distract from your sins." *Sins?!* And the names she called me. You know what Mum can be like when she loses her temper.'

'Spiteful.'

'Vicious. She said things to me that day . . . she said things . . .' Anne stared in silence for a while. 'So can I forgive Mum for that? Can I forgive her for not coming to my wedding? Can I forgive her for refusing to let Darryl step one foot into her flat whenever he drove me there so Liam could see his grandparents? Can I forgive all that? I don't know. As I said, it's not going to be easy.'

'But Mum's not going to the church anymore. You know that. She hasn't been for . . . oh, almost a year.'

'I know, I know. But I think that has more to do with Father Leonard being moved to another parish, than her believing anything *I* told her.'

'Perhaps,' I said.

Anne gave me a little smile. 'Yeah. Perhaps. And on that vaguely conciliatory note . . .' She started to get to her feet. 'Time for bed.' She picked Liam up, and then kissed the top of my head. 'Goodnight, Dom.'

CHAPTER FIFTEEN

I sat on my bed, gazing through the window at the night sky.

The last time I was in this room I had never seen Seb's smile. Or felt Seb's hand in mine. Or admired Seb's white chinos.

And I didn't know about what Anna found in Father Leonard's briefcase, and what Mum said to Anne when she –

'DOM?!'

Billy!

He was calling from his window.

I got off the bed and rushed to mine.

'Shhh!' I said. 'You'll wake everyone.'

'No one can hear me,' Billy said.

'Just keep your voice down.'

'Where have you been?'

'You told me to go away.'

'Not for the whole day.'

'Well, that's what it sounded like.'

'What did you do?'

'Oh . . . things.'

'*What* things?'

'I'll tell you another time.'

'Did you . . . meet anyone?'

Is he jealous?

'I might have done,' I said.

'Who was it?'

'I'll tell you . . . when you write me the next letter.'

'It's written. And posted. Goodnight.'

The letter's in the garden!

I knew Billy would be waiting at his window, wanting to see me rush outside, desperate to get his letter. But I wasn't going to give him that satisfaction.

I'll do some other things first.

I went downstairs and, as quietly as possible, carried the bags of stuff from my old room (that Mum and Dad had brought round) up to my room.

I laid out the notebooks (and sketchbooks) on my desk.

I put some of the paperbacks on my bedside cabinet.

Passages of Joy by Thom Gunn.

The Shield of Achilles by W. H. Auden.

Our Lady of the Flowers by Jean Genet.

I went downstairs again, and out to the moonlit garden.

I walked to the spot where Billy had handed me the first letter.

There it is!

Carefully – avoiding the thorns – I pulled the letter out of the foliage.

A flare of candlelight caught my eye.

Billy was standing at his bedroom window, holding a candelabrum, staring at me.

The candlelight bathed him in an amber – almost golden – glow.

I went back into the house.

I went up to my room.

I put the letter on my desk.

I won't read it yet.

I won't read it yet.

I heard sobbing. Gentle. Just little gasps.

It's Anne.

I went to the doorway.

I gazed into the darkness of the house.

Anne's muffled weeping was like the newly hatched cries of some tropical bird.

This is the story about how Mum fell out of love with working at the Rex.

One day, about nine months after Mum had given the Rex's phone number to the youth on the film crew, Major Vernon rushed out of his office and said, 'I've just had a phone call from Mr Dirk Bogarde's producer! He wants Mr Bogarde's new film, Doctor in the Slums, to premiere here at the Rex.'

Mum waited for Major Vernon to thank her. After all, it was she who'd got word through to the film's producer, as she explained to Major Vernon the day after it happened. But no thanks came.

Mum was too proud to let anyone see – least of all Major Vernon – that it bothered her.

When the local newspaper came to do a piece about the premiere, they interviewed Major Vernon, and he didn't mention Mum at all. Not once. Major Vernon took all the credit. He didn't even want anyone else in the photograph. But Mum insisted that she (and the rest of the staff) be part of it. And the photographer, who'd brought the champagne, agreed it would make a 'more eye-catching' image. Mum claimed it as one small victory. But she didn't want to work

at the Rex anymore. After such a betrayal, who
could blame her? 'I can't stay where I'm not
valued,' she told her mother. 'But I am certainly
<u>not</u> leaving before the premiere.'

Three months later,
the Queen said,
'We'll soon find out
what's in the egg.
Look!'
She pointed to the egg
in the cradle beside the Prince.
The shell was cracking…
cracking…cracking…
And then…a green lizard
crawled out of the egg.

The Queen was afraid the lizard
might bite or claw the Prince,
but when she – or anyone else –
tried to take the lizard
away from the Prince,
the Prince started to cry again.

So the lizard stayed with the Prince.
And it didn't bite or claw him.
Not once.

And, as the Prince got older –
and the lizard got larger –
it became clear to everyone

in the Castle that if the phrase
'best of friends'
could ever be applied to
a royal person and a lizard,
then the Prince and the lizard
were, indeed, the best of friends.

Only ... the lizard was getting
too big to be called a 'lizard'.
One day the Queen said,
'I think the lizard
might be a crocodile.'
And she was right.
It was.

PART THREE

CHAPTER SIXTEEN

Dear Dom,

Where had we got to with our story?

Let me think . . .

That's right!

I'd met Trystan in the zoo.

We'd left the zoo together.

Trystan asked me if I wanted to go back with him and I said I would.

We took a bus. We talked all the way. When we got off, we walked down a long high street.

'That's where I live,' Trystan said, pointing at a boarded-up shop. 'It used to sell records. But business was poor. The manager – Mr Meek – he still rents the rooms above, though. It's a way of having people keep an eye on the place, I suppose. Mr Meek doesn't want squatters. Come on.'

We went through a door beside the shop entrance and up a flight of stairs.

At the top of the stairs there were two doors, facing each other.

'I'm in here,' Trystan said, unlocking the door on the right. 'It's all a bit cramped, but the good news is the person living opposite is away. Travelling. So we've got the whole place to ourselves.'

He ushered me into his room.

It was pretty much as I had imagined it, right down

to the damp patch on the ceiling, and the cracked wardrobe mirror. But there was one thing I had got wrong. The window did not have a Venetian blind. It had a curtain. And there was no green neon coming from outside.

'Would you like a Coke or something?' Trystan asked.

'A Coke would be great,' I said.

He went to the small fridge in the corner.

I was getting an erection just watching him.

He came back with two Cokes, giving one to me.

He raised his bottle, saying, 'To us . . . and all our adventures.'

I said, 'To us . . . and all our adventures.'

This was going to be the first sexual experience I'd ever had any with anyone. I was scared about it happening, but more scared it <u>wouldn't</u>.

That's how I felt with you, Billy.

After it had happened, I felt as if I'd gone through an event horizon to a parallel universe, where everything was the same, and everything was different.

That's it! Yes!

Sex made me what I was supposed to be. Before that night, before Trystan held me and kissed me and said my name, I didn't know who I was. I didn't have an identity. I was just fragments of other people, splinters of other stories, with no narrative of my own.

Exactly! Yes!

I realized now . . . who I love is who I am. Identity comes with intimacy. You can't write the book of yourself until you've opened up to someone else.

Oh, I like that!

I'd been seeing Trystan for a week when he asked me if I wanted to move in with him. I told him I did. We immediately grabbed each other and started kissing and █████████
███
███
███
███
████████████████████████

Why are you editing the sex?!

I used to love watching Trystan get dressed in the morning. He was usually up before me (as he had to get to work at the cinema), and I would just lay back and watch him slip into his T-shirt and white chinos.

White chinos?! Like Seb!

And then — my favourite part — he would style his quiff. He sculpted it with such care and dexterity — combing it, rubbing gel into it, smoothing it with his hands — until it became the gravity-defying coiffure I admired so much.

One morning, Trystan caught sight of my admiring gaze, and asked, 'Thinking about getting a quiff too, Billy?'

'D'you think it'd suit me?'

'No. And I'll tell you why. Because you'll be copying me. This is <u>my</u> "look", not <u>yours</u>. As the writer Gore Vidal said,

"Style is knowing who you are, what you want to say, and not giving a damn." So don't copy me. Discover what <u>your</u> "look" is.'

'I . . . I don't think I have a "look".'

'Of <u>course</u> you do. You just haven't had the opportunity to find out what it is yet.' He sat on the edge of the mattress and held my hand. 'Why don't you let me have a think about it? I'm pretty good at this this sort of thing. And I think I know you better than most.'

'You know me better than <u>anyone</u>, Trystan.'

'Okay. Let's talk about it when I get home tonight.'

I should add that this wasn't the first time Trystan had shown a . . . how shall I say? A lack of enthusiasm about my hair. And the way I looked generally.

He's making you feel insecure.

When Trystan got home from working at the cinema that evening he was fizzing with excitement. 'I know what your hair's got to look like!' he said. 'It came to me like a . . . a vision!'

A vision?!

'Tell me!' I said.

'I'll do better than that! I'll <u>show</u> you.' He held up a small plastic bag. 'In here is everything I need to do your new hairstyle. And, yes, I <u>can</u> do it. You don't need a fancy hairdresser for what I've got in mind. In fact, a fancy hair-dresser would ruin it. They'd make it too slick and polished and . . .' He grabbed me and stared into my eyes. 'Do you trust me, Billy?'

'Of course I do.'

'Then put a towel round your shoulders, sit in that chair, and close your eyes.'

I did as I was told.

Trystan said, 'Don't open your eyes until I tell you. Okay?'

'Okay,' I said.

I felt scissors cutting my hair at the sides. Cutting very close. Then the snipping stopped and . . . what's that? Trystan was rubbing shaving foam over the sides of my head. And then —

Okay, okay, I can see where this is going. Trystan gave you the green Mohican.

I skipped a page.

'Open your eyes,' Trystan said.

I will never forget that moment.

The moment I saw the real me — or, at least, the me with the haircut I was supposed to have — for the first time.

Trystan asked, 'D'you like it?'

I was too emotional to speak. I just nodded.

Trystan started to kiss the shaven parts of my skull, ran his fingers through my green hair and he pushed me onto the mattress and we ███████████████████████████

████████████████████████████████████

████████ then we got in the bath and we ████████

████████████████████████████████████

█████████ spat on his fingers and ████████

████████████████████████████████████

████████████████████████████

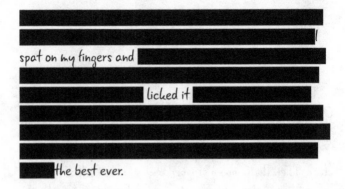

spat on my fingers and

licked it

the best ever.

The missing bits are making me hornier than the bits I can see.

For about a week after Trystan did my Mohican the sex between us continued to be as mind-blowing as that. But then . . . then I felt Trystan pulling away. I asked him what was wrong. He said, 'Your hair is perfect . . . but your clothes! They just don't go with the Mohican haircut. Surely you can <u>see</u> that, Billy!'

He's making you feel insecure again.

The truth was that, yes, I <u>could</u> see it. But I felt awkward about mentioning it. Why? Because I had no money of my own. I wasn't paying Trystan <u>anything</u> towards the rent. Or the food. Or the gas or the electric bills. And I knew that, if I ever <u>did</u> mention it to him, then he would just give me whatever I wanted because he loved me so much and . . . oh, I didn't want to take advantage of him more than I already was.

That's how I feel about living with Anne.

When I explained the reason for my silence, Trystan hugged me and said, 'You're not to worry about <u>any</u> of that, Billy. You're giving me far more than I could <u>ever</u> give you. I'll get you some clothes that you'll really like. Trust me.'

And I did trust him. I trusted him in everything. You understand that, don't you, Dom?

I'm not sure.

The next day Trystan came home with the clothes he'd bought for me. He spread them on the bed: green jeans (torn at the knees), a T-shirt (ripped in places), black boots (with many buckles). But it was the leather jacket that caught my eye. It had been painted to resemble crocodile skin and decorated with ruby rhinestones and golden studs.

The Crocodile Jacket!

I said, 'The jacket is . . . amazing.'

'I just had to get it made for you. It reminds me of some of the crocodiles you've been drawing. The Crocodile Jacket for the artist who loves crocodiles.'

'But it must have cost you a fortune.'

'It doesn't matter, Billy. Nothing matters except making you happy. Put everything on. Let's see what you look like.'

I did as he asked.

'Perfect,' Trystan said, gazing at me. 'Look in the mirror.'

I looked in the mirror.

Again, I was too emotional to speak.

Trystan asked, 'Do you like it?'

Eventually I managed to reply, 'This is . . . the me I'm meant to be.'

<u>The Me I'm Meant to Be</u>. Good title for a song!' He kissed me. 'I just <u>have</u> to take some photos of you! A record of the day you became who you were meant to be.' Trystan got a Polaroid camera from the bedside cabinet. 'Stand by the window. That's it.' He took photo after photo of me, all from different angles. He kept saying, 'Oh, you're perfect . . . oh, you're perfect.'

Didn't you find all this just a tiny bit . . . well, weird?

For about a week or so after Trystan bought me the clothes the sex was mind-blowing once again. But then, just like before, I felt him pulling away.

He wants you to get the tattoos now.

I asked him what was wrong. He said, 'Your hair is just as it should be. Your clothes are just as they should be. But your skin . . . it's too unadventurous compared to the rest of you. It needs something else. It needs . . . tattoos!'

I knew it!

'Tattoos?!' I said. 'Do you really think so?'
'Oh, yes,' Trystan said. 'You need lots of them. On your arms. And some on your chest. And — oh, yes! — a big one down your back. Don't you think so, Billy?'
'Yes,' I said. 'But what should they be of?'

Isn't it obvious?

'Crocodiles, of course,' Trystan said. 'I know a place not

far from here. Let me tell them what you want. Because, as you know, I know you better than you know yourself.'

And so, over the next couple of months, I had

Okay, okay. You got all the tattoos done.

I skipped to the next page.

I'll always remember the evening when all my tattoos had been done and finally healed. Trystan said to me, 'Take off your shirt and stand in the middle of the room.'

I did as he asked.

Trystan got a chair from the table, put it in front of me, and then sat on it.

'Oh, you're so . . . beautiful,' He lifted the front of his T-shirt, revealing his dark, hard nipples. He started feeling his chest . . . his stomach. 'Beautiful . . . beautiful . . .' He unbuckled his chinos and slipped his hand inside.

I stepped forward to touch him.

'No!' he said. 'Just stand there. Don't do anything. I want to . . . to look at you . . . I just want to . . . look.'

He pulled his jeans and boxer shorts down to his ankles, opened his legs wide, and then grabbed his cock and then

████████████████████████████

██████ rub ████████████

█████████████████████ watching me ████

████████████████████████████

█████████████████████████ rub himself

faster █████████████████████████

█████████████████████████████

██████ watching me ██████████████

██████████ watching ████████████

████████████████████████████████████

████████████████████████████████████

rubbing faster ████████████████████████

████████████████████████████████████

████████████████████████████████████

██ spurted and████████

I'm getting really, really horny.

Afterwards, Trystan stood, pulled up his jeans and boxer shorts and kissed me. It was a kiss like we'd never shared before. It was full of such tenderness. Such affection. He put some Dusty Springfield on the record player and we danced and kissed and . . . oh, it was a wonderful evening. The best ever.

I'd love to have an evening like that with Seb.

I can honestly say that the period after this — after my 'look' had been completed — was the happiest I'd ever been. I'd never felt so loved, so cared for, so wanted, so desired.
I wanted it to go on forever.
I thought it <u>would</u> go on forever.
But then the postcard arrived.

The postcard?

The mail was usually delivered early in the morning, while Trystan was still at home (he rarely left for work before midday), so it was always him that went down to collect it. But, on this particular day, the post was late — middle of the afternoon — so it was me who got it.

There was the usual junk mail, a bill, and . . . a postcard. The photograph on the front was of a crocodile in a river. I checked the post mark: the Colombian jungle.

The message was written in blue ink:

> Dearest Trystan,
>   I miss you too. You're right.
>   It is time for me to come back.
>   I will be with you very soon.
>   I can't wait to see you.
>
>   Love
>   Theo
>   XXX

Theo?

It was clearly a previous lover.

And it's clearly not over.

I was tempted to rush to the cinema and confront Trystan with the postcard.

That's what I would've done.

But I waited — oh, that wait felt like a million years — until he got home from work.

'Who's Theo?' I asked, as soon as Trystan stepped through the door, throwing the postcard at his feet.

He picked it up and read it.

I said, 'Why didn't you <u>tell</u> me you were still in love with someone else?'

'I'm not "in love" with him.'

'Well, this Theo — whoever he is — clearly loves you.'
'He loves me but he's not "<u>in</u> love".'

He's playing word games with you now, Billy.

'You're just playing word games now,' I said.
'I'm not!'
'Just tell me. Are you having a relationship with him or not? It's a simple question.'
'And I'll give you a simple answer, Billy. Yes. I have a relationship with Theo. I've <u>always</u> had a relationship with Theo.' He looked me in the eyes. 'Theo's my brother.'

He's never mentioned a brother!

'But . . . you've <u>never</u> mentioned having a brother, Trystan. Not <u>once</u>!'
'I know, I know. It's just that . . . I wanted it to be me and you for as long as possible. And . . . well, Theo had even hinted he might <u>never</u> come back. What was the <u>point</u> of mentioning him if he was never going to be here? But now . . . he <u>is</u> coming back.'
'Well, it was you who <u>told</u> him to come back according to that postcard.'
'I <u>love</u> my brother. Of <u>course</u> I want him to come back. Or should I say . . . I <u>wanted</u> him to come back.'
'Past tense?'
'Yes.'
'Why?'
'Because . . . I'm in love with you, Billy. And Theo . . . if he sees something he wants, he always gets it. Always. And . . . if he sees you and — '

'He will <u>never</u> get me, Trystan.'

'Theo is hard to resist.'

'I don't care. I'll meet him and politely say, 'Welcome back,' and then . . . then I'll never go anywhere near him again. I promise, Trystan. I promise.'

'That's going to be a bit tricky.'

'Oh?'

'The empty room opposite . . . that's Theo's.'

I sense a broken promise looming.

A couple of weeks later, while Trystan and I were in bed watching a late night film on telly, we heard the front door downstairs open and close, and then someone walking up the stairs.

'It's Theo!' Trystan said, jumping out of bed. 'Stay here!'

He poked his head out of the door.

I heard murmuring voices.

Trystan stepped outside.

The murmuring continued.

I turned the sound down on the television.

I heard the door to the room opposite being unlocked and opened.

I heard Trystan say, 'Yes, of course, Theo,' and then the door opposite close.

Trystan came back into our room. He got my jeans and the Crocodile Jacket from the wardrobe. 'You . . . you need to get dressed, Billy,' he said.

'Wh—what for?'

'Theo wants to meet you.'

'Wearing . . . <u>everything</u>?'

'Yes. I . . . I want him to look at you and think, "How did

my pathetic brother get such a beautiful boyfriend?" Please, Billy. Do it for me.'

Don't!

I started to get dressed. I said, 'I'll make him jealous, if that's what you want. But, again, I promise you, I will never — never! — be interested in him. Not while I have you.'

Trystan spent a while preening my Mohican and making sure I was wearing all my jewellery.

'Now knock on Theo's door,' Trystan said, kissing me. 'Go on, Billy.'

I opened our door. I took a step forward. I knocked on Theo's door.

It opened to reveal . . . another Trystan!

What d'you mean?

'Wh—what's going on?' I said, bewildered.

'Hello, Billy,' Trystan's double said. 'I'm Theo.' He looked over my shoulder at Trystan. 'You haven't told him, have you?'

'No, I haven't,' I heard Trystan say behind me.

Theo looked at me and smiled. 'We're twins.'

I could see the room behind Theo. The window had Venetian blinds. There was bright green neon coming from outside. And there was a record playing. It was Elvis Presley singing <u>Love Me Tender</u>.

And that's when I realized . . . I had made a terrible mistake.

The photos I'd found in the photo booth — they weren't of Trystan.

They were of Theo.

Yours Truly.
Billy
XXX

CHAPTER SEVENTEEN

Sunshine.

It's morning!

I'd been up until the small hours reading (and re-reading) Billy's letter. It was still clutched in my hand. My bedside light was still on.

I switched off the light.

I got out of bed and –

> *'Where are you?*
> *Don't you need me anymore?'*

I knew why Billy had started singing. He'd heard me moving about, and now he wanted me to go to him. He wanted me to ask him questions about the letter. And, of course, I *did* have questions. Lots. But – again – I wasn't going to give Billy the satisfaction of knowing he had such a hold over me.

> *'Don't say that's true.*
> *I'll disappear without you.'*

I went downstairs.

A note from Anne was on the kitchen table.

> I'm taking Liam to the park.
> Please do the housework.

Please water the garden.
And DO IT this time!!!
Love
Anne
XXX

P.S.: Phone Mum to say sorry for missing her and Dad yesterday!

I'll call Mum later.
I made some breakfast.

> 'Where are you?
> I have my skin for you to feel.'

Billy was in his kitchen now.
He's following me.
I went back to my room.
I got dressed.

> 'Where are you?'
> I have my story for you to hear.'

I started dusting and polishing Anne's bedroom.
I was glad to have something to keep me busy.
I made Anne's bed.
It was another five hours before I was due to see Seb.
How am I going to survive that long?

> 'Where are you?
> I want you near.
> I want you here.'

He's still following me.

Don't listen to him!

I rushed downstairs.

I went to the garden.

I started fixing up the hose pipe.

I heard Billy's back door open.

He's not going to leave me alone!

I started watering the lawn.

'Morning, Dom,' Billy said.

I didn't respond.

'Dom?'

I didn't respond.

'Why aren't you talking to me?'

I didn't respond.

'Why aren't you – ?'

'You *know* why!'

'I don't. Tell me.'

'You're trying to fuck with my head!'

'And how am I doing that exactly? – Oh! Don't tell me! More coincidences in the letter, I suppose.'

'. . . Some.'

'Such as?'

'White chinos!'

' *"White chinos"*?!'

'The ones Trystan wore!'

'How are they a coincidence?'

Don't reply. Don't engage with him.

'*How* are they a coincidence, Dom? Eh?'

'It's . . . it's nothing,' I said. 'Forget it!'

Billy stepped closer to the foliage. 'You've met someone who wears white chinos! Right?'

I didn't say anything.

'*Where* did you meet them?'

I didn't say anything.

'Let me guess,' Billy said. 'The Rex.'

'Have you been following me?'

'I haven't left the house. But I'm assuming you went there to see if Trystan is – or ever was – an usher. Am I right?'

'You . . . you might be.'

'Of *course* I am. Although *now* you realize . . . it might've been *Theo* who worked at the Rex, not Trystan. Perhaps Trystan worked at another cinema altogether. You'll have to go back to the Rex and ask about Theo now, won't you.' He chuckled. 'Another chance to see those sexy white chinos, eh?'

I threw the hose down and started walking back to the house.

'Wait! Dom! Wait!'

Don't do it!

'*Please*, Dom!'

Don't!

'Dom! I've got something to show you.'

I spun round. '*What?*'

'Come to the end of the garden . . . Come on!'

Don't!

But I did.

I clambered around the remains of the old shed and over the cracked terracotta pots until I was in the shadowy area by the back wall.

The fence was very broken and rickety here, but what remained was held together by an even denser tangle of vines and climbing roses (which were in full, pale pink bloom).

I could just about see Billy through the foliage.

I said. 'What do you want to show me?'

'Step closer.'

Don't!

I did.

I peered through the foliage –

He's unbuckling his belt!

'Not *here*, Billy!'

'Don't you *want* to watch me wank?'

'Someone will *see* you!'

'Only *you* can see what I'm doing.'

'Well, *I'm* not watching.'

'Oh, you *will*.'

He unzipped his jeans.

I looked away.

I heard him moan.

I looked back.

The crimson helmet of his cock was peeping above the waistband of his boxer shorts.

'I'm so horny,' Billy said. 'Touch me, Dom.' He thrust his hips forward. 'Touch me.'

Don't let him play with you like this.

'I'm oozing pre-cum,' Billy said. 'Can you see it?'

Don't let him –

'Yes,' I said.

Billy smoothed pre-cum over the plumb-head of his cock. 'I'm so, so, *so* horny.' He pulled his hand away, a harp-string of spunk connecting his finger to his helmet. 'Touch me, Dom.'

Don't! Don't!

Think of Seb.

Think of –

'*Please*, Dom.' Billy started to thrust his hips more rhythmically, groaning, grinding his cock bulge against his hand. 'Come on, Dom . . . reach through the thorns . . . touch me . . . touch my spunk.'

Walk away.

And, in my mind, I *was* walking away. I was walking

out of the garden, out of the house, and getting as far away from Billy as I possibly could.

But, in reality, I was reaching out and – carefully, carefully! – edging my right hand – my right arm – through the vines and thorns.

'Aww!' A thorn had scratched me.

'Touch me, Dom.'

'Aww!' Another thorn.

I felt the tip of Billy's cock.

'That's it,' he said. 'Feel that spunk.'

Think of Seb!

Think of –

I started to tug his boxer shorts down.

'Oh, that's it,' Billy said. 'Get my cock out.'

Don't! Don't!

Think of –

'Aww!' More thorns scratched me.

Billy's erection sprang out, so bulging with blood it pointed straight up, the helmet almost touching his navel.

'Wank me, Dom.'

I went to grab it.

Billy backed away.

I pressed myself into the foliage.

Thorns scratched my face.

'Wank me,' Billy said.

'I . . . I can't reach far enough to . . . do that.'

'Then you'll just have to come inside the house, won't you.' Billy was turning away, walking towards his back door. 'We can spend the rest of the day making each other cum and – '

'No, Billy!' I said. 'You're just trying to distract me from seeing Seb – '

'*Aha!* So *that's* his name!'

'Shut up!'

'Seb in the sexy, white chinos!'

'Shut up! Shut up!' I started clambering back over the shed and pots.

'Dom!'

'Leave me alone!'

I went into the house.

I went up to the bathroom.

I cleaned the scratches on my arm.

I put my shoes on.

I left a note for Anne.

I've gone to see Seb.
I might be back late.
Don't worry.
Love
Dom
xxx

I rushed – ran! – out of the house.

Billy was standing in the open window of his downstairs front room. He was holding a guitar. Like the Crocodile Jacket, it had been painted to resemble crocodile skin.

'You haven't seen the Crocodile Guitar yet.' Billy said, lifting it in the air. 'Come and have a look! I've written a new song. It's called *Crocodiles in Your Eyes*. The title you came up with. Remember?'

I kept walking away.

Billy called, 'I'll play it for you.'

'Fuck off, Billy!' I called back.

CHAPTER EIGHTEEN

'Dom!'

'Hello, Seb.'

'What're you doing here?'

'I'm sorry, I'm sorry. I know I'm early. *Very* early. And I know we agreed I'd come round to your flat at four o'clock, not here at the Rex at two. But I've been having a shitty day. A really, *really* shitty day. And I just had to see you. Because you're the only one in the whole world who could make it *not* shitty. And, yes, I know it sounds like a stupid thing to say because we've only known each other for . . . what? A day? Less! And, perhaps, I've got no right to just barge in here like this and say, "Please turn my shitty day into an unshitty day." Perhaps you're looking at me and thinking, "I wish this needy nerd would go away." And perhaps I *should* go away and – '

'Calm down, calm down. I *want* you here.'

'You . . . *do?*'

'Of *course* I do. My day's been pretty shitty too. Why? Because I've been missing you for every second of it. That's after I spent a whole night dreaming about – What happened to your face? It's all scratched. *And* your right arm.'

'Oh . . . I . . . I was pruning some roses . . . and they fought back.'

'Your own little Wars of the Roses, eh?'

'Yeah. And the roses won!'

'I'll get you a consolation Coke. Why don't you go over to our table. I'll join you in a second. Okay?'

'Okay.'

I'm feeling calmer already. Why did I let Billy get to me like that? I'll never let it happen again. Seb's all that matters now. And I love the way he referred to this table as 'our table'.

'Voila!' Seb was walking towards me, a Coke in each hand. 'Cheers!' He gave me a bottle and sat down.

'Cheers!' I said.

We clinked bottles and drank.

I will not ask him to check if Theo ever worked – or works – here. I'm not bothered about anything Billy tells me anymore.

I won't ask him.

I won't ask –

'Seb ... can I ask you do something for me? And I know this is going to sound ... a bit stupid. *Worse!* Ridiculous! But ... well ...'

'Just *ask*, Dom.'

'Okay. Is the manager here? – What's his name again?'

'Mr Ellroy. He's on the roof,' Seb said. 'Decided he wanted to do a bit of sunbathing. I said to him, "Be careful! You're almost as fair-skinned as I am. Any longer than thirty minutes in this weather and you'll burn to a crisp." So I've got to go up and tell him to stop in ...' Seb checked his wristwatch. 'Seven minutes.' He stared at me a moment. 'You've got another question you want me to ask him, haven't you.'

'Yes.'

'Let me guess. About someone *else* who might've worked here.'

'... Yes.'

'Okay. Who is it this time?'

'Someone named Theo. Theo Finch.'

'Finch? The same surname as the Trystan you asked about?'

'They're brothers.'

'. . . I see.' Seb frowned and smiled simultaneously. 'Okay. I'll ask.' The frown disappeared, but the smile remained. 'And are you going to explain *why* you want to know if – ?'

'Yes. Later. Promise. Okay?'

'Okay.' He gave me a quick kiss on the cheek. 'Time for me to get on with things. Including asking the manager about this Theo Finch. Feel free to pop in and out of any films you like. Or you can read my *Life of King Edward II*. I should warn you, though. It does *not* end well.'

'I think I'd rather just sit here and watch you.'

'Damn! I *knew* I should have washed my hair last night.'

I watched him as he served at the box office. I watched him as he let a few people into Screen Two. I watched him as he rushed up to the roof, and then, a few minutes later, rushed back down and called over to me, 'No Theo here!'

I felt foolish for even mentioning Theo now. And the more I watched Seb the more foolish I felt.

At five o'clock Seb finished work.

We walked down Bethnal Green Road together, making our way to where Seb lived.

Seb said, 'So . . . Trystan and Theo. Who are they?'

I had been expecting the question, of course, and had spent most of the afternoon trying to work out how to answer it, without actually lying.

I didn't, for example, think it a good idea to tell Seb I'd only met Billy Crow earlier that week. And – an even worse idea – to reveal Billy was living next door to me.

I said, 'Oh, it's just that this person I met once – '

'You mean the guy you had a relationship with?'

How did he guess that?!

I said, 'Well . . . yeah. This guy happened to mention that he knew two people who worked in a cinema, and I thought, "Wouldn't it be a coincidence if one of them – or both of them – worked at the cinema where *you* worked?" That's all.'

'And this ex – whoever he is – never told you name of the cinema?'

'No.'

'And you never bothered to ask?'

'. . . No.'

Seb did the smile 'n' frown thing again. 'Okay. Fine.'

I reached out to hold his hand.

Seb didn't take it at first, and then he did.

We walked in silence for a while.

'Oh, this is my favourite shop!' Seb said, pointing.

It was a small, second-hand shop called Yesterday's Treasure. I'd seen it before, but always walked straight past. Now, Seb was pulling me over to look in the window. It was full of tatty furniture, bits of jewellery, moth-eaten clothes, broken toys, and faded photographs from another era.

'I bought my bedside cabinet here,' Seb said. 'It's solid oak. Edwardian. Cost next to nothing. Do you want to go inside and have a rummage?'

'If *you* want to, sure.'

'Well, *I* only want to if *you* want to.'

'Well . . . to be honest . . . I'd rather get back to your place so we can . . . rummage with each other.'

Seb grinned. 'In that case . . . let's get going.'

We started walking again.

Seb said, 'I only mentioned Yesterday's Treasure

and the cabinet because ... well, I want to tell you everything about me. It's like I've taken a drug called *Tell Dom Everything You've Ever Done*.'

'I feel the same about you!'

'Really?!'

'Yeah!'

'Great!' He pointed. 'That's the opticians where I get my eyes tested!'

'My turn!' I pointed. 'See that lamppost! When I was about nine years old I wasn't looking where I was going and – whack! – I walked straight into it.'

'Ouch!'

'I had a bump on my forehead for weeks – And there! That's the newsagents where I used to get my Spider-Man comics.'

'I used to buy my Spider Man comics there too!'

'You like Spider-Man!?'

'I *love* Spider-Man. And the X-Men.'

'Oh, I like X-Men as well.'

'Who's your favourite?'

'Cyclops.'

'Mine too. Eyes that can burn the thing he loves. It's like a story Oscar Wilde could've written.'

'I'd love to see what Oscar Wilde would've done with an X-Men story.'

'Oh, yes! An angel? Skintight spandex? He'd've had a field day.'

And we talked like that – everything we looked at provoking some memory about ourselves – all the way to Seb's block of flats.

It was five storeys high and made of pale yellow brick.

'The lift has broken down,' Seb said, 'so we'll have to walk up.'

'Didn't you say you were on the top floor?'

'Afraid so – Come on! I'll race you!'

We ran up the stairs.

Seb got to his landing first.

'It's not fair,' I said, breathlessly joining him. 'You're *used* to doing this.'

'I've got good leg muscles,' Seb said.

'I'd noticed.'

'Really?' He grinned. 'You can feel them if you like.'

I squeezed his thigh.

'Very firm,' I said. 'Feel mine.'

He squeezed my thigh.

'You're firm too,' he said.

'I'm firm . . . in lots of places.'

'Then we'd better get to my room pronto – Come on! This way!' He led me along the landing. 'I used to ride a skateboard up and down here.'

'You had a skateboard?!'

'It was Rory's. That's my brother. He let me use it. I was pretty good at it.'

'Those strong leg muscles, eh?'

'I'll give you a demonstration later on.'

'Of the skateboard or your leg muscles?'

His grin grew wider. 'Both if you like.' He stopped outside a front door. 'And here – ta-dah! – is my "humble abode", as the saying goes.'

We went inside.

The furnishings (and general decoration) were not dissimilar to my parents' taste (sofa, two armchairs, heavily patterned carpet, floral wallpaper). The main difference was the television (a much bigger screen), the hi-fi system (sleeker, with state-of-the-art speakers) and the row of professional-looking cameras on the coffee table.

'Mum moved here when Rory was a toddler,' Seb said, 'so most of what you see is hers. When Mum died the council let Rory take the place over. He's five years older than me. Rory used to be my legal guardian too. But, believe me, *I've* always been the grown-up in *that* particular relationship.'

'I'm *very* impressed by all the cameras. I can see the Nikon FM. That's the camera *I* want.'

'They're all Rory's. He takes photos of weddings and stuff. That's his job.' He held my hand. 'Shall we go to my room?'

'I thought you'd never ask.'

His bedroom looked a lot like mine: shelves of books and records, a single bed, small wardrobe, desk in the corner.

'Well?' Seb pointed at his bedside cabinet. 'What do you think?'

'I like it,' I said.

'Be honest!'

'Well . . . I'm sure I'll *grow* to like it.'

Seb laughed.

I said, 'Let's start rummaging.'

I stepped towards him.

Seb stepped back.

'What's wrong?' I asked.

'You're still seeing him aren't you?'

'Who?'

'The guy who told you about Trystan and Theo. The one you told me you weren't seeing.'

'I . . . what makes you think I'm still – ?'

'I'm not an idiot, Dom.'

'I didn't say you –'

'Why didn't you ask me about Trystan and Theo at the same time? I'll tell you why. Because this guy you're still seeing – the ex-boyfriend who's clearly not an ex – only told you about Theo . . . when? Last night? This morning?'

I sat on the edge of his bed.

I said, 'Okay. I'm sorry. But, honestly, I haven't actually *lied* to you, Seb. I told you the relationship was over and that's the truth. I give you my word.'

'But you met him again?'

'. . . Yes.'

'When?'

'This morning. Briefly.'

'Why?'

'Because . . . he's a very manipulative person. He's got a sort of hold over me. It's hard to explain.'

'Try.'

'He tells me things. And these things . . . they sort of play on my mind. They're *meant* to play on my mind.' I grabbed his arm. 'Seb! I'm going to ask you a question. And I know it's going to sound a bit weird and paranoid but I'll ask it just once to get it out of the way and then I'll never – '

'Just ask, Dom.'

'You sure?'

'Ask!'

'Okay, okay . . . Do you know someone named Billy Crow?'

'That's the ex, I presume.'

'Yes.'

'No. I don't know him.'

'Perhaps you met him . . . in passing. A casual conversation in a pub or something. No names exchanged. He's got a green Mohican haircut and – '

'Stop right there! I have *never* had a chat – casual or otherwise – with *anyone* with a green Mohican.'

'You're sure?'

'I think I'd remember.'

'You might have met him *before* he had his Mohican. He used to wear – '

'Shush, shush!' Seb held my hand. 'Listen, Dom. This Billy Crow – whoever he is – doesn't sound like a particularly nice piece of work. Forget him. It's just us now. Okay? *Us.*'

'. . . Thank you.' I squeezed Seb's hand. 'I promise I shall never mention – or even think about – Billy Crow ever again.'

'Cross your heart?'

'Cross my heart.'

'Good!' He smiled. 'You can rummage me a little if you like.'

I wrapped my arms around him, buried my face in the nape of his neck, and inhaled.

This is what safety smells like.

I could feel Seb's hands going up and down my back, exploring the ridges of my spine as if they were Braille.

I started to kiss him.

My tongue touched his tongue.

I put my hand between his legs and –

'Whoa, whoa!' Seb held my wrist. 'Not so fast.'

'But I thought you wanted to – '

'I *do*. We *will*. But we don't have to rush things. Listen. My brother's got a new girlfriend and he's spending most of his time at her place. We've got the flat to ourselves. For the whole night. So let's . . . let's take our time. Okay?'

'. . . Okay.'

'What about a bite to eat?! You hungry? I am. Starving. Luckily, I'm great in the kitchen. How'd you fancy . . . I'm thinking of what's in the fridge . . . I can rustle us up an asparagus and tomato frittata. And there's half a quiche Lorraine left from last night. And I can make us some Caesar salad to go with it! Followed by . . . fresh peaches and ice cream!'

'My mouth's watering already!'

'And – I've just had another idea! Ready?'

'Ready!'

'Why don't we have it on the roof? It's brilliant up there. Especially when the weather's like this. You'll love it. Sound good?'

'Sounds perfect.'

'Let's do it!'

CHAPTER NINETEEN

'The view's amazing!' I said.

'I know,' Seb said. 'Careful!'

We were on the roof. I'd gone as close to the edge as I dared (there was a parapet, but it didn't seem quite high enough to prevent a fall).

I said, 'Are we . . . *allowed* to be up here?'

'To be honest . . . no. Not really.' He spread a blanket and started putting the food (in Tupperware containers) onto it. 'There used to be a sign on the roof door saying "NO ENTRY". But someone ripped that off years ago. I think it might have been Rory. Actually, I'm pretty sure it *was* Rory.'

'So . . . it's not really safe?'

Seb chuckled. 'Well, no one's fallen off yet. And, as the writer William Burroughs once said, "When you see a door marked "NO ENTRY", it's your duty to walk straight through it." – Come on! Let's eat!'

I sat beside him on the blanket.

Seb handed me a plastic plate, knife and fork, and then, indicating the food, said, 'Help yourself.'

We started eating.

'This is *really* good!' I said. 'Where did you learn to cook like this, Seb?'

'Mum. I was always in the kitchen helping her – Do you want some more coleslaw?'

'Yes, please.'

He forked some onto my plate. 'Rory took some wonderful photos of Mum up here. It was her birthday. Rory had bought Mum a kite. He always buys whacky stuff like that. He's like a big kid. We came up here to fly it. The sun was shining but it was a tad chilly. My favourite kind of weather.'

'Mine too.'

'Mum let go of the kite and – whoosh! It was off. Up, up, up to the clouds. Mum held on to the string tight as she could and . . . oh, how she laughed. We *all* did. When I think of Mum now . . . I like to think of times like those. You know? The happy times. Because . . . well, me and Mum – we had lots of arguments. Not serious ones. Petty ones. Stupid. We just . . . clashed sometimes.'

'I clash with my mum too. Big time.'

'Then you've got to stop it, Dom! One day she'll be gone and you'll regret all the nasty things you said. You'll regret it and you won't be able to tell her you're sorry.' He started to cry. 'And that's a horrible feeling, Dom. Horrible.'

I wrapped my arms around him.

I could feel his breath against my cheek.

I could feel his heart against my chest.

'It's okay,' I said. 'It's okay.'

I want to cry too.

'Goodness!' he said, pulling away, wiping his face on a serviette. 'What's wrong with me? I invite you up here for a jolly picnic, and then I start blubbering all over your shirt.'

'It's fine.'

'It most definitely is *not* fine – Hang on! That sounds like Rory!' He jumped up and looked over the edge of the roof. 'It *is!* – RORY! UP HERE! I'M WITH DOM!'

He's told his brother about me!

I heard his brother yell something.

'YEAH!' Seb yelled in reply. 'BRING YOUR GHETTO BLASTER WITH YOU!' He rejoined me on the blanket. 'Thought we could do with some music – You don't mind me asking Rory up, do you? He's dying to meet you. You'll like him. His new girlfriend's with him. I've only met her a couple of times. She seems really nice. Easy to get on with. And – oh, yeah. Don't mention anything about my mum dying. I know you probably wouldn't but . . . well, Rory doesn't handle serious stuff too well. With Rory, you have to keep everything as light and jokey as possible. To be honest, it's a relief to have someone like that around. Well, *most* of the time – Let's make some room for them!'

We shuffled ourselves – and moved the food – to one side of the blanket.

'READY OR NOT, HERE I COME!' a voice boomed from the stairs leading up to the roof.

Seb said, 'Rory's pretty much on full volume all of the time. You'll get used to it – Hello, Rory!'

'Hello, you two! Hope you're not doing anything to scare the pigeons.'

Rory was like a louder, dayglow version of Seb: his hair was more canary yellow than platinum, his physique more rugby player than swimmer, and his smile a little too exaggerated to feel entirely disarming.

He swaggered up to us, put the ghetto blaster down, and then, indicating me, said, 'So this is him, eh?'

'It is,' Seb said. 'Dom, this is my brother – Rory. Rory, this is Dom.'

'Pleased to meet you, Rory,' I said.

'Ditto, Dom.'

We shook hands.

Rory indicated the scratches on my face and arm. 'How'd you get those? Not from my little brother here, I hope – ha, ha, ha!'

'No,' I said, attempting a laugh.

'Or perhaps,' Rory went on, 'perhaps you had a fight with a pack of kittens – ha, ha!'

Seb said, 'He's been pruning roses, if you *have* to know. And it's a *litter* of kittens.'

'Only if they're born together,' I said. 'Otherwise it's a kindle of kittens.'

'Ooo, I like that!'

'You can say an *intrigue* of kittens too.'

'The alliteration of "kindle" is better.'

'I agree.'

Rory said, 'You two have lost me.'

'Where's your new sweetheart got to?' Seb asked.

'She's titivating herself in the bathroom. Crash helmets do catastrophic things to a perm – You got anything to drink up here?'

'Yeah, here!' I passed him a can of Coke.

'Thanking you!' He gulped it down, liquid spilling from the corners of his mouth. 'That's better!' He wiped his lips. 'Riding a motorbike's thirsty work in a heatwave.' He looked at me. 'I'm glad little brother's met you, Dom. Life can be a lonely thing if we haven't got a huggable amigo – And talking of which! Here's mine!'

His girlfriend had just walked onto the roof.

I know that face!

'Come here, beautiful!' Rory put his arms around her. 'Ooo, you smell nice.' He looked at me and Seb. 'She's been using my aftershave again – ha, ha, ha!' He kissed her. 'Let me introduce you to my little brother's recently discovered – and recently rose-scratched – huggable amigo. Dom, this is Zoë. Zoë, this is –'

'Dominic!' Zoë said, staring at me. 'Is that you?'

Zoë! My sister's one-time best friend!

Seb said, 'You two *know* each other?'

I said, 'Zoë used to . . . go to school with my sister.'

'How is Anne?' Zoë asked. 'I haven't seen her in ages.'

'She's fine. Her *and* Darryl. They're both *very* happy.'

'Oh . . . well . . . that's good. And little Liam?'

'He's great.'

'And has Anne learnt to drive yet?'

'She going to start lessons soon.'

'I remember she was super keen to get a car of her own.'

'Well . . . things have been a tad busy, I expect.'

'Yes . . . yes, of course.' She gazed at me a moment. 'And *you!* You've grown up *so* much since I last – '

'THIS IS A BORING CONVERSATION!' Rory boomed, turning the ghetto blaster on. 'TIME TO BOOGIE!'

CHAPTER TWENTY

We danced on the roof for nearly two hours.

Seb had tuned the ghetto blaster to a new radio station he was keen on, Rainbow Live, and the first thing we heard was the DJ say, 'And now our Saturday night Summer of Love Collection,' and then ... *Stayin' Alive* started to play, and we all cheered and started disco dancing (with Rory doing a pretty good John Travolta impersonation), and then *You're the One That I Want* came on (and I attempted a – not so good – John Travolta, partnered by Seb who, I have to say, made a pretty gobsmacking Olivia Newton-John), and we were all laughing and boogieing and generally having a good time as one classic after another – *Love Is the Drug* by Roxy Music, *Rapture* by Blondie, *Don't You Want Me* by The Human League – took us towards sunset.

Rory – being Rory – did more than just dance, of course. Apart from impersonating Travolta (and Freddie Mercury and Boy George), he juggled with Coke cans, walked on his hands, and sang *Rocket Man* while standing on the parapet.

Zoë watched Rory with the look of someone who hadn't yet decided if she found his antics endearing or maddening. Probably, like me, she found them a bit of both. Once or twice, I caught her smiling at me, trying to establish some kind of kinship, and I smiled back, but all the time I was thinking, *You're the person who stopped*

*talking to my sister because you were jealous of her going out
with Darryl. You were Anne's best friend. How could you do
that to her?*

When Bowie's *Wild Is the Wind* started playing
everything slowed down, and we all smooched as we
danced.

As the song came to an end, Rory said, 'All the food's
gone and I'm still starving! Who fancies a takeaway
pizza? And perhaps something stronger to drink? Beer
or something?'

Seb and I said we were fine with the Cokes, but a pizza
did sound like a good idea.

Zoë wanted a pizza, and wouldn't mind some shandy.
'And perhaps some more crisps.'

Which prompted Seb to say, 'And you'd best get some
more Cokes while you're at it, Rory.'

Which prompted Rory to say, 'Then *you'd* best give
me a hand, little brother. I can't carry it all.'

'Okay.' Seb looked at me. 'What pizza do you want,
Dom?'

'Whatever you're having,' I said.

'That's love!' Rory pointed at me and Seb. 'Ha, ha, ha!'

'Leave them alone,' Zoë said.

'I'm just having fun!'

'Well, sometimes what *you* consider fun is just ...
bullying.'

Rory looked like something slimy had just been
thrown into his face, and he wasn't quite sure how to get
it off. And then, suddenly, the look disappeared, and he
said, brightly, 'Yeah! Okay! Sorry – ha, ha, ha! Come on,
brov.'

Seb rolled his eyes at me and followed his brother off
the roof.

I sat on the blanket.

Zoë sat next to me.

She said, 'How *is* Anne? *Really?*'

'As if you're bothered,' I said.

'Of *course* I'm bothered.'

'Oh, sure. You're *so* bothered you stopped talking to her just when she – '

'I did no such thing!'

'Anne told me all about it, Zoë!'

'*What* did she tell you, exactly?'

'About you and Darryl.'

'Go on.'

'You fancied him. You got jealous – '

'Okay, okay, I've heard enough!' She looked around, double-checking we were alone. 'I'm going to tell you what really happened. But on one condition. You never tell Anne that you know. You never tell *anyone*. Okay?'

'I . . . I don't know what you – '

'Just shut up and listen! First! I did *not* stop talking to Anne. It was *Anne* who stopped talking to *me*. Second, it had *nothing* to do with me fancying Darryl. Why? Because I did *not* fancy him. Darryl wasn't – *isn't!* – my type. I like my boyfriends to tell *me* how beautiful *I* am now and again, not constantly ask *me* how beautiful *I* think *they* are. Also, I like them to be fun. I like them to have a sense of humour and make me laugh. Now, that's not to say I took an instant dislike to Darryl or anything. I didn't. When me and Anne met him on the beach that day, I thought he was friendly enough. Not bad looking, sure. But – I repeat! – Not. My. Type. Is that clear?'

'. . . Yeah.'

'I could tell that Darryl was instantly besotted with Anne, of course. So he should be. She was well out of his league. Intelligent, well-mannered, sophisticated. Everything he's not. What *did* surprise me was how besotted *she* was with *him*. When they started "officially" going out I was – yes, I admit it – shocked. It shocked a lot of people. I bet *you* were shocked, right?'

'I . . . I don't remember.'

'Well, your *mum* was shocked. I doubt you've forgotten *that*. Your mum said to me, "Zoë, that boy will be the ruin of Anne." Not the most original line, but that doesn't mean it wasn't true. Your mum always assumed – like I did – that Anne would marry some studious, ambitious type. A teacher. Or a chief librarian. She used to have a crush on John Boy from *The Waltons*, for heaven's sake! Your mum asked me to have a word with Anne. A sort of "make her see the error of her ways" chat. And I *did* talk to Anne. A few times. Not in a heavy way. But in a best friend "I hope you're totally sure this is what you want" sort of way. And each time I asked, Anne said that yes, she *was* sure. She was totally sure and she was totally happy. So, eventually, I let it go. Naturally, I was upset when Anne quit school. Not just because she wouldn't be taking her exams, but because it meant I'd be seeing her even less. But . . . these things happen. You have to be grown up about it. And Anne and me – we still had our long chats on the phone. And it stayed that way until . . .' Anne took a gulp of Coke. 'I went to see a film at the Rex. I'd planned to go with my mum, but she went down with one of her migraines so . . . well, I ended up going by myself. I was in the queue, waiting to buy a ticket, when I heard a voice say, "Well, look who's here!" It was Darryl. He'd been walking past and spotted me. He said he was seeing Anne later and he had a few hours to kill and so – if I didn't mind – he'd see the film with me. What could I say? So we bought our tickets. Darryl wanted to pay for mine but I insisted – *insisted!* – I pay for my own.' Another gulp of Coke. 'The film had only been on a few minutes when I felt Darryl rubbing his leg up against mine. So slowly, so gradually, I didn't think anything of it at first. Perhaps he was trying to get comfortable in his seat. I moved my leg away. The next thing I know, his hand's on my leg! *High* on my leg! And getting higher. I got up and walked out of the cinema. He chased after me. "What're you getting into such a bloody huff about?" he said. "I know you want it, Zoë. I thought we could . . . you know. A little fun before things get *too* serious between me and Anne." I said, *"Before* they get *'too* serious'!? Anne's pregnant with your baby, Darryl. The two of you are getting married next week. How much *more* serious do you want?" I walked away from him. He didn't follow. I wanted to forget about the whole thing. But then I thought, if Darryl could do that with me – Anne's best friend – who's to say he's not doing it with other women? And would *continue* to do it. Was this *really* the kind of person Anne wanted to spend the rest of her life with? To bring up her child? And so . . . I told her. And Anne . . . she called me a liar. She said Darryl had already told her I was making eyes at him. Lies! All lies! Me and Anne had a blazing row. She told me I would not be welcome at her wedding, and that she never wanted to see me again.' Zoë took a deep breath. 'I did try to . . . to heal things between us. I sent her little notes. I phoned. For weeks I did this. Months. Anne ignored every –'

'DRINKS AND PIZZAS AHOY!'

Rory and Seb had arrived back on the roof.

Zoë pulled me close. 'Don't forget,' she said, softly. 'Keep what I've just told you to yourself. If Anne and Darryl are happy – there's no point it digging it all up now.'

CHAPTER TWENTY-ONE

By the time we'd finished the pizzas, stars were beginning to sparkle.

Seb and I were lying on the blanket, pointing out constellations, while Rory and Zoë canoodled against the parapet.

'I could call in sick in the morning,' Seb whispered in my ear.

'Eh? What?'

'The Rex. I'll call and say I'm sick. I only work the evening on Sundays anyway.' His hand was working up my leg. 'That means ... after we've spent the night together, we can sleep late in the morning, very late, and then have all day together, and then we could spend *another* night together.' He kissed my neck, my cheek, my lips. 'Think of all the rummaging we could do.'

'Yeah,' I said.

But, as soon as he'd finished suggesting it, another thought had popped into my head.

What if Billy's left me another letter?

Rory and Zoë came over to us.

'Me and Zoë are making a move,' Rory said. He looked at Seb. 'Do you want a hand taking everything off the roof, brov?'

'No, no. Me and Dom can do it.'

What if there's a letter in the garden right now? What if I'm not back tonight? Anne might find it. Darryl might find it.

'Okay.' Rory said, giving Seb a hug. 'Hope all the

dancing hasn't tired you out for ... the sultry night ahead – ha, ha, ha.'

'Just go, Rory,' Seb said, smiling.

We all said our goodbyes.

What if Billy's letter is found by animals? A dog? A rat? A cat? What if they gnaw and peck and claw it to pieces?

Seb and I started taking the Tupperware, ghetto blaster, and everything else back down to the flat.

Seb was talking to me about his brother. Did I like him? Yes, I did. He didn't ruin the evening for you, did he? No, he didn't.

Billy will never write me another letter if this one gets ruined. I'll never know what happened between him and Trystan and –

Did I like Zoë? Yes, I did. Such a coincidence, her knowing your sister, eh? Yes, it is.

Billy's letter will be found or get ruined.

Billy's letter will be found or get ruined.

Billy's letter will be found or get ruined.

We went back to the flat.

Seb closed the front door.

Billy's letter will be –

'Alone at last!' Seb said, smiling.

'What? Oh. Yeah.'

Seb started to kiss me.

I kissed him back but –

Billy's letter will be found or get ruined.

'Let's go up to my room.' Seb said.

'Okay, yeah.'

We went to Seb's room.

Seb started to unbutton my shirt. He was more passionate than he'd ever been. He kissed my nipples. He started unbuckling my jeans and –

'Wait, wait,' I said.

'What's wrong?'

'I . . . I'm not in the mood.'

'You're . . . *not*?'

'I . . . I'm sorry.'

'Have I . . . have I done something wrong?'

'No!'

'If I have, tell me and I'll – '

'You haven't done *anything* wrong, Seb. Honestly. It's just me.'

'Do you still . . . want . . . *us*?'

'Of *course* I do.'

Seb thought for a moment, and then said, 'Okay. We can just snuggle up and watch telly and – '

'No, I . . . I think I want to . . . go.'

'Go?'

'. . . Yeah.'

'As in . . . *not* staying the night?'

'I'm sorry, Seb. It's been a brilliant evening. The best ever. Honest. But . . . it's just that . . . oh, I don't know. My head's all over the place. Please say you understand. *Please*.'

Billy's letter will be found or get ruined.

'Okay, okay,' Seb said. 'I think I understand . . . Or perhaps I don't, but . . . well, if that's what you want . . .' He kissed me gently on the cheek. 'Come on. I'll walk you to the bus stop.'

'Thank you.'

Billy's letter. Billy's letter. Billy's letter.

Billy's letter. Billy's letter. Billy's letter.

Billy's letter. Billy's letter. Billy's letter.

The bus came along as we neared the stop.

I kissed Seb quickly, and then rushed to get on the bus.

'Phone me tomorrow,' Seb called.

'I will,' I called back

'In the morning.'

'Yeah.'

'Early!'

'Yeah!'

I got on the bus and sat by the window.

I waved at Seb as the bus pulled away.

Billy's letter. Billy's letter.

Billy's letter. Billy's letter.

Billy's letter. Billy's letter.

Billy's letter. Billy's letter.

When the bus arrived at Bow – my stop! – I jumped off the bus and ran –

Billy's letter.

Billy's letter.

Billy's letter.

The street was still and empty when I got there.

There was candlelight in Billy's room.

I rushed into Anne's house.

All the lights were off.

Everyone's asleep.

I turned on the light in the kitchen.

I made my way to the garden.

Quietly, quietly.

I walked – carefully, carefully – to the spot where –

A letter!

So it hadn't been found.

It hadn't been ruined.

Carefully, I pulled it out of the foliage.

I noticed a glimmer of light out the corner of my eye.

Billy's watching me from his bedroom.

I did not look up at him.

I went back into the house.

Anne, wearing her nightdress, was coming down the stairs.

'Was that you opening and closing the back door?' she asked.

'Oh . . . Yeah,' I said. 'I just popped outside to see if . . .' *Think quick, think quick.* 'To see if I put the hose away before I left this morning.'

'You didn't.'

'Sorry.'

'And I've no idea what you consider to be housework, but I saw no sign you'd actually done any.'

'I dusted your bedroom and made your bed.'

'And not much else!'

'. . . Sorry, Anne.'

'You've been with this Seb again, I suppose.'

'Yeah.'

'While I've been here all day. Alone with Liam.'

'I thought Darryl was coming back.'

'He did. He had a bath and went straight to bed. Not much company to be had there.'

'Sorry, Anne. I'll make it up to you.'

'You will. Tomorrow. I've invited Mum and Dad round for Sunday dinner.'

'You *have*?!'

'Well, Mum phoned and suggested we all have it together and . . . well, Darryl will be in a better mood if it's on "home turf". It'll be the first time he's seen Mum since Liam was born.'

'Is it *that* long?'

'It's *that* long. I've taken a joint of beef out of the freezer. And a sherry trifle for afterwards. And I'll say to you what I said to Darryl. If you're not there tomorrow I shall kill you.'

'I'll be there. Promise. Can I ask Seb to come?'

'If that's what it takes to guarantee your presence, of course.' She sighed. And then she smiled. 'No, seriously, *please* bring him. I'd love to meet him. And he might help keep the atmosphere more . . .'

'Relaxed?'

'Convivial.' She looked at me a bit closer. 'Are those scratches on your face and arms?'

'Oh . . . yes . . .' *Think quick, think quick!* 'The cinema's got a pet cat now. It's had kittens. They were a bit frisky.'

'Put some antiseptic on them before you go to bed. The scratches, not the kittens.' Anne started making her way up the stairs. 'You heard the weather forecast?'

'No.'

'A storm's on the way apparently.'

'We always get one of those after a heatwave.'

'Well, let's just hope it holds off until *after* we've all had dinner. *That's* likely to be stormy enough as it is.' She shook her head ruefully. 'What *have* I let myself in for?'

This is the story of how Mum and Dad met.

For a few days after the article about the Dirk Bogarde premiere appeared there was a constant trickle of people coming into the Rex and asking for tickets. Mum explained – with ever-decreasing patience – that the premiere was a private event (the film studio had bought all the seats) and, therefore, no members of the public would be able to attend. Eventually, Mum made a sign saying 'DIRK BOGARDE PREMIERE – SOLD OUT!' She was putting it up outside when she heard a voice behind her say, 'Oh, what a shame.'

Mum turned to see a young man wearing a slightly crumpled suit and highly polished shoes.

'I'm sorry,' Mum said. 'It's a VIP event.'

'I can imagine,' the man said. 'I think Dirk Bogarde is such a wonderful actor. Did you see him in A Tale of Two Cities?'

'Yes, I did. He was so ... noble.'

'He was, wasn't he?'

Mum's sign was in position now, and there was no reason for her to stay outside, except that there was something about the young man's clear complexion and fruit bat eyes that made her linger.

'Your suit needs ironing,' she told him, for want of something to say.

'Oh, I know. It's been in the wardrobe for over a year. I've been away, you see. I work on a farm.'

'Really?'

'Yes. In Norfolk. I was evacuated there during the war and ... well, I just sort of stayed on. I've come back because my sister isn't very well and –'

A rapping on the glass door of the cinema. Major Vernon was calling Mum back inside.

'I must be going,' Mum said to the young man. 'Lovely talking to you.'

'And you.'

Mum went back into the cinema, but looked back at the young man. And the young man was looking back at her.

A couple of days later Mum was in the canteen at the London Hospital when she heard a voice say, 'Hello, again.'

It was the young man with fruit bat eyes.

'Oh! Hello,' Mum said.

'Can I join you?'

'Yes, yes, please do.'

He sat down and smiled. 'I've ironed my suit.'

'So I see. It was awfully rude of me to mention the creases. I'm sorry.'

'Oh, I don't mind.'

'I like your tie.'

It was maroon with white stripes.

'Thank you,' he said. 'My sister bought it for me. Last week. Birthday present.'

'How old were you?'

'Nineteen.'

'Same as me. Well, in a couple of months.'

He smiled. 'You look very ... grown up.'

'So do you.'

'Do I? My sister always says I've got a baby face.'

'I don't think that at all. You remind me of the actor Farley Granger. Do you know him?'

'No.'

'I saw him in a film about the writer Hans Christian Anderson once. I don't usually like musicals, but I liked that one. And Farley Granger looked lovely in it.' Mum sipped her tea and dunked a biscuit. 'Don't your parents miss you? Being away on the farm so much.'

'They're both dead.'

'Oh, I ... I'm so sorry.'

'It's fine. Well, it's not fine but ... I never really knew them, you see. Dad left us a month before I was born. So I <u>say</u> he's dead, but - of course - he might not be.'

'But he's dead to you.'

'That's right. And my mum ... well, she was killed by a doodlebug during the war. Two days

before she was due to join me and my sister in
Norfolk.'

'So your sister – she came back to the East
End after the war?'

He nodded. 'She's a lot older than me. She had
a fiancé. He was in the army. When he came back
home – to Whitechapel – my sister joined him and
... well ... that's it really.' He sipped his tea
and dunked a biscuit. 'It's my sister who's in
the hospital.'

'What's wrong? If you don't mind me asking.'

'Something to do with her heart. They say it's
serious. I don't know what I'd do if anything
happened to her. She's all I've got really.' His
fruit bat eyes brimmed with tears. 'I'm sorry.'
He looked away, reaching for his handkerchief.

For the first time since she'd been a child
Mum wanted to hug another person.

The young man wiped the tears from his face.

'I can get you a ticket,' Mum said. 'For the
premiere.'

'You ... you can?'

'All the staff get one ticket each. I'll be
working, so I'll see the film anyway. It's a
shame to let the ticket go to waste.'

'But there must be someone else you want to
ask?'

'Not really. Well, there's my mum. It's her I've
just been visiting. The doctors say she's got
something wrong with her blood.'

'She might recover by the time of the – '

'No. She won't. Please have the ticket.'

'Well ... thank you. But you must let me pay you
for it.'

'It didn't cost me a penny.'

'But . . . I want to give you <u>something</u>.'

'Why don't you take me out for dinner afterwards?'

'Oh! Really?'

'Don't you <u>want</u> to take me out for dinner?'

'Yes! Of <u>course</u> I do. I'd like that. Goodness, I don't even know your name.'

'Marian,' Mum said.

'I'm Lionel.'

Lionel came to the premiere wearing a new suit and the tie Mum liked so much. Afterwards they went for dinner at Pellicci's.

Six months later Lionel asked Mum if she would marry him.

A week later Mum said, 'Yes.'

Needless to say,
everyone in the castle
was worried that the crocodile
~ as it got bigger and bigger ~
might eat the Prince.
But the crocodile
didn't seem to show
any interest in the Prince
as a potential dinner.
Indeed, the friendship between them
~ if not love ~
grew stronger
and stronger.

When the Prince was thirteen years old
he said, 'My crocodile is

the most beautiful thing in all the land.
And I want to make it even more beautiful.
Bring me emeralds and diamonds.
Bring me rubies and pearls.
Bring me gold.
I want to decorate it.'
The Prince's orders
were obeyed at once
(of course they were).

The Prince pressed
emeralds and diamonds
and rubies and pearls
into the skin of the crocodile.
And he covered its claws with gold.
And when the Prince
walked round the Castle ~
with the glittering crocodile
on a silk leash ~
he felt as if he were
the most powerful person
in the whole land.

And then,
when the Prince was eighteen,
the Queen died,
and the Prince actually became
the most powerful person
in the whole land because
he was now the King.
The King said to the crocodile,
'We shall be Kings together,
you and I.'

PART FOUR

CHAPTER TWENTY-TWO

Dear Dom,

how are things going with Seb?

Don't bring Seb into this, Billy.

Have you kissed him yet? I mean really, <u>really</u> kissed him? I suspect you have. But have you gone further? Have you unbuckled those sexy, white chinos of his? Have you rubbed his cock and sucked him? Have you done all the things that we do?

Things we did, Billy! Past tense.

I suspect you haven't.

Just tell me about Theo!
I skipped a half a page.

For a moment, I just stood there, gazing at Theo as he stood in the doorway to his bedsit, and Trystan — Theo's identical twin — stood behind me in the doorway to his.

Theo looked over my shoulder at Trystan and said, 'He's ... amazing.'

Trystan said, 'Look at his eyes, Theo. Green.'

'They're perfect.' Theo touched my hand. 'Do you want to come in for a while? We can . . . get to know each other. Would you like that?'

I said, 'I'd like that a lot.'

I went into Theo's room.

I didn't even glance behind me to look at Trystan. It was as if Trystan didn't exist anymore. All I could think of was Theo.

The thing Trystan feared the most has happened. Theo has stolen you from him.

'Trystan told me you've had some tattoos done,' Theo said, as soon as the door closed behind me.

'I have.'

'Show me.'

I took the jacket off and showed him the tattoos on my arms.

'Show me <u>all</u> of them,' Theo said.

I took off my T-shirt.

Theo walked around me as if I was an artwork in a museum. 'Flex the muscles in your back so the crocodile moves.'

I flexed some muscles.

Theo ran his fingers over my skin.

I said, 'So . . . you've been to the Colombian jungle?'

'That's right.' Theo stood directly in front of me, so close I could feel his breath on my lips.

'It must have been . . . an adventure,' I said.

'It was.' He lay his hand on my chest. 'A terribly big one.'

I was getting hard, and it showed.

'Did you see any crocodiles?' I asked.

'I did.'

'That must've been . . . exciting.'

'It was . . . but not as exciting as this.' He kissed me.

I wrapped my arms around him and kissed him harder.

Needless to say, I stayed in Theo's room that night and we ▮▮▮▮ and ▮▮▮▮ and ▮▮▮▮.

I'm getting turned on again.

I was woken next morning by the sound of Trystan's door opening and closing, and him rushing down the stairs, slamming the front door behind him.

Theo stirred beside me. 'What was that?'

'Trystan. Going to work.'

'Work!? What a horrible thought.' He propped himself up on an elbow and gazed down at me. 'All I want to do is stay here with you.' He went to kiss me but —

'I'm worried about Trystan,' I said.

'Why?'

'What d'you mean "why"? I've been going out with him all this summer. It's been good. We've been happy. And now — '

'Don't worry about it.' Theo kissed my neck. 'Trystan's a grown-up. Besides, he's used to it. We might be twins but everyone's always fancied _me_ the most.'

'How many "everyones" have there been?'

'I don't want to talk about the past, Billy. It doesn't matter anymore. All that matters is you and me — us — here and now. You should go to Trystan's room and take out any stuff that belongs to you and bring it here.'

I don't think I like this Theo very much.

There wasn't much to take. A few clothes (socks, jeans, T-shirts, underwear), a couple of paperbacks, and my sketchbooks.

Theo became immediately interested in my sketchbooks. He flicked through them, murmuring, 'Oh, these are good . . . *very* good . . .' He pointed at one. 'Tell me about this!'

It was of crocodiles swirling against a star-filled sky.

I'd always found it hard to talk about my drawings and paintings.

So have I.

But Theo kept coaxing me, asking questions, until I did manage to say something: I told him that the image first came to me in a dream. I saw all the colours and everything. I used watercolours because I wanted the greens and blues to be as luminous as possible.

'Like stained glass windows,' Theo said.

Exactly.

'Exactly!' I said.

No one had ever talked to me about my art like this before. Yes, Trystan had said he liked my drawings when we first met, but — after that — his comments became fewer and fewer, until they disappeared altogether.

But Theo . . . oh, Theo could talk for hours and hours. He told me about what artists my work reminded him of (and thus what artists I should look at), and all the ways my images could be improved and developed.

Theo encouraged me to be more ambitious with the images too. He said, 'These sketchbooks are far too small for your ideas. I'll get you some bigger ones.' And he did. Bigger and bigger. And when they were too big to put on the table Theo cleared an area of wall for me so I could stick sheets of paper onto it.

'You need to be freer with the paint,' Theo told me. 'This size is far too large for watercolours. I'll get you some tubes of acrylic paint. And bigger brushes. You should look at the some photos of all the graffiti going on in New York. Murals. It's amazing.'

The one thing he did keep saying to me was, 'At least you've found your subject.'

Crocodiles.

I painted all day, every day. I couldn't wait for Theo to get back home from the cinema (yes, he'd started working at the cinema again by now) so he could see what I'd done. He always gasped with delight as he came through the door and caught sight of what I'd been doing.

That must have been a wonderful feeling.

One day, when I'd done a painting so big it was spilling off the paper and onto the wall, Theo said, 'I've got an idea!' He searched in his bedside cabinet. 'I don't know why I didn't think of it sooner! — Aha! Here it is!' He held up a key. 'Follow me.' He opened the window.

'What're you doing?'

'Going downstairs. It's quicker this way.' He climbed onto the fire escape. 'Come on!'

I knew the fire escape was there, of course, but it had always looked too old and rickety to actually use.

'Downstairs . . . to _what_?' I asked.

'Somewhere that'll be opened . . . by _this_!' He held the key up again. 'Come on.'

'Is the fire escape . . . safe?' I asked.

'Of course it is.' He started walking down the metal steps. 'You coming or not?'

I climbed through the window and followed him. The whole fire escape clanged and quivered around me.

It was late autumn now, and the nights were drawing in.

I called. 'Where're you taking me, Theo?'

He called back, 'The record shop used to hire out an empty room. For bands to rehearse in. I was in charge of it.'

'You used to work in the record shop?!'

'Yeah. Me _and_ Trystan. Didn't he tell you?'

'No.'

'I got a job first. Then I persuaded Mr Meek — that's the manager and — '

'Your landlord. Trystan _did_ tell me _that_.'

'Well, he gave my brother a job in the shop as well. We were quite an attraction. "The Finch Twins". We played up on it. Dressing more and more alike. No one could tell us apart — Hurry up, Billy!'

Theo had reached the bottom of the fire escape and was walking across a small courtyard. He went up to a large door. The door had a small window in it.

I rushed down the final flight of steps and joined him.

Theo unlocked the door, pushed it open, and then went inside. 'Come on, Billy!'

I followed him.

It was dark.

'Where's the bloody light switch got to?' I heard Theo mutter. 'I haven't been here for a while . . . Eureka!'

The lights came on.
And I gasped.

What did you see, Billy?

The room was about forty or fifty foot square. There were no windows and there was no furniture (except for an electric bar fire in the corner). But there were paintings. Lots of them. Over the ceiling and three of the four walls. Paintings of —
'Crocodiles,' I said.
They were disconcertingly three-dimensional and ablaze with colour (shades of viridian and emerald green for the epidermis, cadmium red — with red rhinestones — for the eyes, and glittering gold for the claws).

Just like your paintings, Billy.

'They're amazing!' I said. 'Who did them?'
'One of the bands who used to rehearse here.'
'Why haven't you shown them to me before?'
'Perhaps I was waiting for you to be ready.'
'For what?'
'Painting something this . . . epic. As you can see, there's one wall left. You can paint it, Billy. Take inspiration from all that's around you.'
'<u>Copy</u> it, you mean?'
'Well, the style's very close to yours anyway. Don't you think?'
'Yeah . . . yeah, I do.'
'And besides, as Andy Warhol once said, "All art, like life, begins as impersonation."'

I ran my fingers over the crocodiles. 'I feel like I could grab hold of them.'

'In some places you almost can. See? The texture of the wall — all the bumps and ridges and cracks in the plaster — they've been used to give the crocodiles depth and make them look . . . alive.'

'What're they painted with?'

'Spray paint.'

'I've never used that.'

'But you like the look of it, right?'

'Yeah. I like it a lot.'

Theo put his arms around me. 'I can get you all the spray paint you need. _And_ I can get you red rhinestones and gold leaf.'

'This is _real_ gold leaf?' I reached out for a claw.

'It is. Oh, Billy . . .' He kissed my neck. '_This_ is what your art should look like. _This_ big. _This_ bold. _This_ . . . amazing! Take inspiration from it. If you make a mistake, it doesn't matter. You can just keep painting over it until you get it right.' He kissed me on the lips and felt between my legs. 'Perhaps you can paint . . . a jungle scene. How's that sound? Good? _I_ think so.' He was unzipping me now and reaching for ███████ 'And perhaps there can be . . . hummingbirds. Small as thimbles and glittering like jewels. And a lagoon. And in the middle — under the surface — the shape of a crocodile. Huge. "The Crocodile God".'

The Crocodile God?

From that day on, I had a new regime. I would spend the morning making sketches, and then spend the afternoon in the rehearsal room, transforming the sketched ideas into paintings on the wall.

Theo was, as always, as good as his word, and got me all the spray paint (and red rhinestones, and gold leaf, and anything else) I needed.

Lucky you!

At first, I found using the spray cans difficult. I made lots of mistakes, so there was a great deal of painting over. But, after a week or so — and with a lot of studying the crocodile paintings that were already there — I began to master the technique.

Theo was eager to see what I was doing, of course, but I banned him from the rehearsal room. I said, 'You can't see anything until I'm ready to show you.'

That's what I would say.

One night, after I'd been working late in the rehearsal room, I went back to the bedsit to find Theo already in bed.

The clunking of the fire escape had woken him.

'Sorry,' I said. 'I didn't realize it was so late.'

'Nothing to apologize for. I want you to paint. I bought us some pizzas. Do you want me to warm yours up?'

'No. I just want to lie here beside you.'

I took off my clothes. I got into bed.

'I know you don't want me to see anything yet,' Theo said, 'but . . . can you describe what you're doing down there?'

'Well . . . it's only just beginning to <u>really</u> come alive but . . . there's a lagoon in the background. And there's a large crocodile in the middle.'

'The Crocodile God!'

'Yes.'

'Oh, that sounds <u>very</u> exciting.' Theo started rubbing his cock.

'And the Crocodile God is surrounded by smaller croco-diles.'

'Oh, yes, yes.' He was fully erect now, thrusting his hips.

I went on, 'And they all link together, shape fitting into shape, so that, from a distance, it could be an abstract pattern. And there's hummingbirds and —'

Theo grabbed my ███████████████████

███████████████████████████████████

███████████████████████████████████

███████████████████████████████████

███████████████████████████████████

███████████████████████████████████

███████ sucked and licked ███████████

███ I cried out louder and louder and —

Suddenly there was banging on our door.

It's Trystan!

'It's Trystan,' I said.

'Stay there!' Theo got out of bed, put some clothes on, and opened the door.

I caught a glimpse of Trystan outside. He looked dis-traught.

'Can't you at least have sex <u>quietly</u>?!' I heard Trystan say. 'For <u>my</u> sake? Eh?'

'Shhh, calm down,' Theo said. 'It's okay.'

'It is <u>not</u> okay. I've tried not to say anything before. But this! Tonight! It's too much!'

'Let's talk in your room. Come on.'

They went into Trystan's room.

I got up and crept to the door, eavesdropping.

They were talking too low for me to hear most of it, but I did manage to catch Trystan say, 'He was mine before he was yours.' And Theo replying, 'I know, I know, but that's your fault, not mine.' And then the talking stopped and it was replaced by the sound of Trystan sobbing.

Trystan must be going through hell.

I went back to bed. About ten minutes later Theo returned and joined me.

I asked, 'How is he?'

'Everything's fine.'

It's far from fine!

I told Theo, 'I hate to think of Trystan upset like this. And it's all my fault.'

'You mustn't think like that, Billy! You and me are made for each other. You know that. Trystan knows it too. It's just jealousy on his part. He's going to have to get over it. Everything will calm down soon enough.'

I bet it doesn't.

And, after that, yes, things did seem to calm down.

Really?

But only because Theo and Trystan stayed out of each other's way. Up until then, on most days, they went to work together and came home together. But, now, Trystan left earlier, hours before the cinema could possibly be open, and he came home later, much later, hours after the cinema must have closed.

Trystan can't bear to be in the same house as you and Theo. Listening to you and Theo being so happy together. Listening to you have sex.

The times I liked best with Theo were the evenings, after dinner, when (if I wasn't painting too late) we'd turn the lights down low, and Theo would play records. He had a large collection, and he liked a lot of different things (not just Elvis Presley and rock 'n' roll, though that — of course — was the major part of it).

Theo introduced me to music I'd never heard before. Some I liked, some I didn't. Theo always encouraged me to be honest about what I thought and, more importantly, explain why. He said to me, 'Working out what we <u>don't</u> like is just as working out what we <u>do</u>.'

Again, I'd love to have an evening like that with Seb.

One night he pulled an LP off the shelf, and a single fell out along with it.

'So <u>this</u> is where it got to,' Theo said, picking up the smaller record. 'I've been looking for it everywhere.'

'What is it?' I asked.

'It's one of the best songs <u>ever</u>,' he said. 'You've got to hear it!' He put it on the record player.

The record was a bit scratchy. A guitar started to strum. And then a voice started to sing.

'The sky will be a different sky
The sun will shine like new.'

That's the first song I heard you sing, Billy! At least the words are the same.

'Who is it?' I asked Theo.
'A band called Crocodiles & Cadillacs.'
'I've never heard of them.'
'Hardly anyone has. They paid to have this record made themselves. They did a few gigs in pubs and then . . . it was all over. They disappeared — Oh, listen to that chorus, Billy!'

'I am the change you want to be.
So be it, be it, be it.
I am the change you want to see.
So see it, see it, see it.
Oh, see it, see it, see it.'

'Catchy, eh?' Theo said.
'Very.'
Theo started to sing along.
'You sing too!' he said.
I started singing with him.
'You've got a good voice, Billy,' he said.
'Really?'
'Yeah. Sing louder.'
I sang louder.
When the record came to an end, Theo played it again, and then again, each time encouraging me to sing with more confidence and

Okay, okay. I get it. Theo encourages you to sing. He buys you a guitar. You learn to play. You paint it so it becomes the Crocodile Guitar. What next?

At last! The painting in the rehearsal room was finished!

I took Theo down to see it. His eyes became wide — and moist with tears — as he looked round.

I'd painted not just the remaining wall, but the whole of the ceiling too. The join between the old painting and mine was seamless. In some instances I has continued painting crocodiles onto the floor.

Theo said, 'It's like the Sistine chapel of crocodiles.'

That's what you called your ceiling, Billy.

Theo started to kiss me and unbuckle my

I skipped a page.

The next day Theo and I decided to have a romantic dinner in the bedsit to celebrate the completion of the rehearsal room mural (or The Crocodile Room, as we had started to call it).

Theo cooked a

Not interested in that.

And there was a candelabrum on the table and

Not interested in that either.

Halfway through the meal Billy took something from his pocket. It was wrapped in green tissue paper.

'This is for you,' he said, handing it to me.
'What is it?'
'Open it and see.'

I bet it's a ring.

It was a ring.

In the shape of a crocodile?

It was gold, and in the shape of a crocodile. The eyes were red gemstones.
'There's an inscription,' Theo said.
I looked on the inside of the ring.

'To My Only Love From Your Only Love.'

Theo said, 'I love you, Billy. You're the only one I will <u>ever</u> love. If you feel the same about me, put the ring on.'
I put the ring on.
We kissed.
'Champagne!' Theo said. 'We need champagne! Why didn't I think of it before?!' He jumped to his feet. 'I'll get some now.' He put his jacket on. 'I won't be long!' He rushed out of the room.
I heard him run down the stairs.
I heard him run out of the house.
The front door went, SLAM!
The candles quivered.
I gazed at the ring on my finger.
'So he gave it to you, then?'
I spun round.

Trystan was in the still-open doorway.

'You're home early,' I said.

'It's started to snow. A blizzard's on the way. All non-essential staff told to go home. That's what I am. Non-essential.' He stepped into the room. 'Having a nice romantic dinner, eh? Very cosy.'

'Let's not argue, Trystan.'

He indicated the ring. 'Theo <u>told</u> me he was going to give you that. And you put it straight on. No hesitation, eh?'

'Please don't —'

'I still love you, Billy. I can't help it. I promised Theo that I'd try to stop. And I <u>have</u> tried. But I can't do it. It's not possible.' He stepped closer.

'Trystan —'

'It's not your green hair I love. Or your tattoos or . . . or the clothes you wear. It's <u>you</u> I love. The essence of <u>you</u>.'

'And Theo <u>doesn't</u>. Is <u>that</u> what you're saying?'

Trystan stared at me a moment. 'You don't have any idea what's been going on, do you?'

'Wh–what do you mean?'

He took a wallet out of his jacket pocket. 'I wasn't going to show you this.' He removed a photograph from the wallet. 'But now . . . now I feel I have no choice.' He held the photo out. 'Look!'

I took the photo from him.

It was of Theo and me. I had the green Mohican. I was wearing the Crocodile Jacket. Tattoos were visible through rips in my T-shirt. We were both standing outside the record shop. The record shop was open. It was strange to see its window full of records and posters.

Only . . . I hadn't known Theo (or Trystan) when the record shop was open.

That's not you in the photograph, Billy.

I looked at Trystan. 'Who . . . who is it with Theo?'

'Kalvin,' Trystan said. 'Kalvin Sparrow. He and Theo were <u>so</u> in love. I'd never seen a love like it. When Kalvin died I thought Theo would lose his mind. It was me who suggested Theo travel for a while. See new things. And he did. He went to the Colombian jungle. But Theo's state of mind didn't improve. His postcards home started to scare me. Theo said he might never come back. I was worried he would . . . kill himself. And so I did what any brother would . . . I tried to save him. I tried to give him another Kalvin.'

And that's when I realized . . .

Those photos Trystan had taken of me after I'd had all the tattoos done — he'd sent them to his brother.

I was the lure.

The lure that brought Theo back from the jungle.

Yours Truly.
Billy
XXX

CHAPTER TWENTY-THREE

'Hello?'

'Seb?'

'Yeah.'

'It's me. Dom.'

'Well . . . good morning.'

'I'm not phoning too early, am I?'

'Not at all. And I will now lose all credibility by saying I've been sitting by the phone *waiting* for your call. In fact . . . I was beginning to worry you might *not* call.'

'Why would you think that, Seb?'

'Oh . . . I'm just a natural born worrier.'

'It's because I left early last night, isn't it?'

'Early . . . and so *suddenly*. Dom, are you *sure* I didn't do anything wrong?'

'No! You were . . . perfect. *Everything* was perfect.'

'I kept thinking . . . what if he doesn't want to see me again? What will I do without him?'

'I feel the same, Seb. Truly. Which is why I'm going to lose all credibility myself and ask you the following question. How do you fancy having Sunday dinner with us?'

'With you and Anne and – ?'

'With me and Anne and Darryl and Liam and – wait for it! – my mum and dad.'

'The whole clan, eh?'

'*Please* come, Seb. Anne really wants to see you. And . . . well, I don't think I can get through it without you by my side.'

'Then it's my *duty* to be there.'

'I should warn you, though. This dinner's a bit of a . . . well, a sort of reconciliation.'

'Between . . . ?'

'My mum and Anne mainly.'

'Because? Don't tell me if it's private and – '

'No, no, it's fine. It's over Darryl.'

'Mum doesn't approve of her son-in-law, eh?'

' "Doesn't approve" is a bit of an understatement. So I can't guarantee the atmosphere's going to be all smiles and sunshine. I'd understand it if you didn't want to – '

'I wouldn't miss it for the world. What's your address?'

I told him, and then gave him directions.

'What time shall I turn up?' he asked.

'Dinner's at two so . . . half past one?'

'Perfect. See you later. Bye.'

'Bye.'

I glanced at my wristwatch.

It's four hours till I see Seb.

Anne called me from the kitchen.

I went to her. 'Seb'll be joining us for dinner!'

'Good – What're you doing?'

'Making some toast.'

'You've *had* breakfast.'

'I'm still hungry.'

'There's no time for second helpings. We've got the whole house to tidy. *And* a roast to cook. And – oh, yes! I want you to lay the table. It needs your artistic touch.'

I could see Darryl playing with Liam in the garden.

I asked, 'Is *Darryl* going to help at all?'

'Hopefully not. He'll only confuse things.' She watched Darryl through the window. 'Look at him. Trying to be a good dad. Let's see how long *that* lasts . . . Okay! Let's get this show on the road.' She took the joint of meat from the fridge and put it in a roasting tray. 'Every time I cook a roast dinner – which hasn't been *that* often, I admit – I always think, Mum used to do this every single Sunday. I know she still does but, when me and you were kids, she'd have to give us breakfast, wash us and get us dressed, not to mention doing all the housework *and* looking after Dad when he was ill. You remember how exhausting *that* could get?'

'He couldn't even go to the toilet by himself.'

'And Mum did it all. Without a word of complaint. Without making any fuss at all. And – what makes me blush with shame now – Mum did it all without receiving a word of thanks or a –'

'YOU BLOODY IDIOT!' Darryl shouted in the garden.

'MUM!' Liam screamed.

'Oh, what's happened *now*?' Anne muttered.

Darryl stormed into the kitchen.

'He's messed up my quiff!' Darryl said.

'He's a *child*, Darryl.'

'I told him not to touch my hair. I *told* him!'

Darryl rushed upstairs to the bathroom.

Anne watched him go and then sighed. 'Well,' she said, 'the "good father" act didn't last long, did it.' She put the beef in the oven. 'Dom, you start doing the housework upstairs, I'll do down here. Once I calm Liam down.'

I tidied my room first. I made sure Billy's latest letter was tucked (along with the others) at the back of the bedside cabinet drawer.

It's three and a half hours till I see Seb.

I finished tidying my room and then made a start on Anne's.

I imagined the moment Seb would knock at the front door. I'd rush to open it and, when I saw him, I'd say, 'It's great to see you, Seb' and he'd say, 'It's great to be here, Dom', and we'd hold each other and –

'What're *you* doing here?'

Darryl was standing in the doorway.

His quiff was gleaming.

I said, 'I'm making the bed.'

'That's mine and Anne's bed.'

'I do *know* that, Darryl.'

'So you know it's private, right?'

'I've made it before.'

'When?'

'When you weren't here.'

'What's *that* supposed to mean?'

'Nothing. I was just saying that I – '

'I've got to go out to work, you know.'

'I know, I know.'

'It's not *my* fault if that work makes me "not here" for days.'

'I know, Darryl, I – '

'I'm the only one in this house who *does* work. Who d'you think pays for all the food you're eating. You're not paying us a penny in rent. Nothing!'

'I thought all this was agreed! I'll get a part-time job once college starts – '

'DARRYL!' Anne called up. 'YOU OUT OF THE BATHROOM?'

'YEAH!' he called back.

'THEN KEEP AN EYE ON LIAM. I CAN'T DO ANYTHING WITH HIM HANGING ONTO ME. PUT A "DO NOT TOUCH" SIGN ON YOUR HAIR OR SOMETHING!'

Darryl mumbled something and went downstairs.

I finished Anne's room and then started cleaning the bathroom.

It's two hours till I see Seb.

I imagined taking him up to my room, closing the door behind us, and kissing him and –

'DOM?'

'YEAH?'

'YOU FINISHED UP THERE?'

'JUST ABOUT.'

'START LAYING THE TABLE.'

'OKAY.'

I went to the dining room and started laying the table.

I'll show Seb my typewriter. I'll show him all my favourite books. I'll show him my drawings. I'll show him –

'MUM!' Liam screamed.

I heard Darryl yell, 'SHUT UP! SHUT UP!'

I went to the dining room doorway, just as Anne was rushing out of the kitchen and into the living room, where Darryl and Liam were.

'Stop shouting at him, Darryl!' she said.

'He won't do anything I tell him – Look what he's done to my hair! Again!'

'MUM!'

'It's all right, darling.' She picked up Liam, glaring at Darryl. 'You've got to have patience.'

'I *have* got patience,' Darryl said. 'But he pushes it too far, the little bastard.'

'Don't you *dare* call your son that!'

'Oh, it's all *my* fault now, is it? Eh? What *is* this? Let's All Pick On Darryl Day or something?'

'Don't be so childish. Go and cool off somewhere. *Go on!*'

Darryl looked lost and flummoxed for a second.

'I . . . I'm going to do my quiff.'

'It looks fine!' Anne said.

I said. 'And I've just done the bathroom.'

Darryl ignored us and went upstairs.

Anne kissed Liam. 'Shush, shush, love. Everything's okay.' She looked at me. 'Table done?'

'Yeah.'

'Let's have a look.' She went to the dining room. 'Oh, that's lovely, Dom – Hasn't Uncle Dom made the table look nice, Liam?'

'Yeah!' Liam said.

Anne kissed me on the cheek. 'Come on! Let's get dinner started.'

It's an hour till I see Seb.

We were halfway through preparing all the vegetables when Darryl strode into the kitchen.

'What've we got to drink?' he asked.

Anne said, 'We've got water, lemonade, bitter lemon and Coke.'

'No wine?'

'None of us drink, Darryl.'

'*I* do.'

'I'm well aware of that.'

'What's *that* supposed to mean?'

'Nothing, nothing.' Anne sighed. 'I just thought ... today ... for the sake of keeping everything calm and peaceful ... we could all just have water or – '

'We can't have dinner without wine!'

'We've *never* had wine with – '

'We've got guests! It's different!' He went into the hallway and picked up his car keys from the console table. 'I'm going out to get some.'

'DARRYL!' Anne called.

But he left the house, slamming the door behind him.

We heard him pull away like he'd just robbed a bank.

'Why's he in such a bad mood?' I asked.

'He's terrified,' Anne said.

'About seeing Mum?'

'About . . . everything.' Anne sighed. And then, brightly, 'I'm going to get changed. You can finish here. That okay?'

'That's fine.'

She went upstairs.

It's thirty minutes till I see Seb.

I finished preparing the vegetables.

I gave the table one last check.

Fifteen minutes till I see Seb.

I put the potatoes in the oven.

I gave the table another last check.

Ten minutes till I see Seb.

I took the beef out of the oven.

Five minutes.

I washed my hands.

Three.

I checked my hair.

Two.

I checked my hair again.

One.

Where is he?

It's half past one.

He should be here by now.

I opened the front door.

I looked down the street.

I can't see him.

I came back into the house.

He's not going to come. He doesn't want to see me anymore. How am I going to get through dinner? How am I going to get through the rest of my fucking life –

A knock at the door.

I opened it.

Seb said, 'Sorry I'm a bit late, Dom. I took the wrong turning and – '

I kissed him. Hard. Long.

'Well!' Seb said, when my lips had finally left his. 'That's the sort of welcome I could easily get used to.'

'I thought you weren't coming,' I said.

'Why on earth would you think that?'

'Oh . . . I'm just a natural born worrier.'

'Well, I'm here. And – Ta-dah! – I've bought some flowers.' He held out a small bunch of roses.

'Thank you,' I said, ushering him into the house.

'They're for Anne.'

'Oh. Of course. She'll love them.'

'*What* will I love?' Anne was coming down the stairs, carrying Liam.

I said, 'Anne, this is Seb. Seb, my sister, Anne, and my nephew, Liam.'

'Nice to meet you, Anne,' Seb said. And then, looking at Liam, said, 'And nice to meet you too, buddy.'

Liam smiled.

'And these,' Seb went on, holding out the flowers, 'are what – hopefully – you will love.'

'I *do* love,' Anne said, putting Liam down and taking the bunch. 'Thank you.'

'Thank *you* for inviting me.'

He's saying all the right things. And he's so relaxed. I can tell that Anne likes him.

My fingers felt for his fingers.

Anne's noticed.

'Why don't you show Seb your room,' Anne said, giving me a smile. 'I'll finish getting dinner ready.'

'You sure?' I said.

'Absolutely.'

I took Seb up to my room.

My fingers were feeling more than just his fingers now.

And his fingers were feeling more than just mine.

We kissed . . . and kissed . . . and kissed . . .

I started unbuttoning his shirt.

He started unbuttoning mine.

'You're sure this won't ruin our appetite?' Seb said.

'You're right,' I said. 'Perhaps we shouldn't get too carried away.' I started buttoning up his shirt.

He buttoned up mine.

'Oh, I like all these layers of wallpaper,' he said, looking round the room. 'Image on top of image.'

'I like it too. The bottom layer of wallpaper – the one with the roses on – that must be seventy years old or something.'

'You know what it reminds me of? Joe Orton's room. You know Joe Orton?'

'The playwright. Of *course* I do.'

'Of *course* you do. Well, his boyfriend – '

'David Halliwell.'

'Ten out of ten! Halliwell covered their bedsit walls with a collage of photographs he'd cut from magazines and things. Have you seen it?'

'No.'

'It's *totally* brilliant!' He continued looking round. 'And look at all your books.' He knelt besides the piles of paperbacks on the floor.

'I haven't got any shelves yet,' I said. 'Darryl was supposed to get me some this week but . . . well, he hasn't been around much and – '

'*Giovanni's Room* by James Baldwin! I've got that. It's brilliant. *Leaves of Grass* by Walt Whitman. Of *course*.'

'Of *course*.'

'*A Streetcar Named Desire* by Tennessee Williams – Have you seen the film?'

'It's amazing.'

'Marlon Brando in that sweaty T-shirt!'

'Marlon Brando *without* that sweaty T-shirt!'

'Sexiest thing ever.' He continued looking at the books. 'Lots of Christopher Isherwood, I see. I've read *Goodbye to Berlin* at least three times. It's not his best work, though.'

'I agree. That's – '

'*A Single Man*,' we said together.

We both laughed.

Can Billy hear us laughing?

I opened the window a bit wider.

Seb said, 'And *Les Enfants Terribles* by Jean Cocteau. I haven't read *anything* by him.'

'I'll lend you some books. He's a visual artist too. Have you seen his film, *Orpheus*?'

'No.'

'It's mind-blowing. Sexy hunks on motorbikes representing death – '

A knock on the front door.

I said, 'That'll be my parents.'

We listened as Anne let them in.

I said, 'We should go down.'

'Ready when you are.'

I held his hand.

I said, 'Mum'll make some comment about me wearing black. You watch.'

We went downstairs.

Everyone was in the living room.

'There he is!' Mum said, looking at me. Then added in the same breath, 'Who's funeral you going to?'

I looked at Seb.

He grinned.

Mum's eyes locked on Seb. 'And who's this?'

'It's my friend Seb,' I told her.

'He's joining us for dinner,' Anne said.

'Seb, this is my mum. And dad.'

'Hello, Dom's mum and dad,' Seb said, smiling.

His smile's on full blast!

Mum said, 'I'm Marian and this is Lionel.'

'Hello, Marian. Hello, Lionel. Nice to meet you both.'

'Nice to meet you too,' Dad said.

Mum looked at me a bit closer. 'Where'd all those scratches come from?'

'He played with some frisky kittens,' Anne said.

'Kittens?' Mum looked at Anne. 'You've got kittens?'

'No,' Anne said. 'They were at the Rex.'

'The Rex?!' Mum said. 'You went to see a film at the Rex *in this heat?*!'

'That's what *I* said,' Anne said.

'And what're kittens doing at the Rex anyway?'

I said, 'The Rex has got a cat, Mum. For mice.'

'Well, it never had mice when *I* worked there.'

Seb – who obviously had no idea how this 'kittens at the Rex' topic had come about – was still happy to join in. 'Oh, there's plenty there now, Marian,' he said. 'In fact we're thinking of getting *two* cats.'

' "*We're* thinking"?'

'Seb works at the Rex, Mum,' I said.

'Dom told me you organized the Dirk Bogarde premiere.'

'I did,' Mum said. 'I arranged *everything*. And then I was stabbed in the back.'

'It happened a long time ago, love,' Dad said.

'It feels like yesterday to me, Lionel. But I won't go into it all now.' She looked at Seb. 'I did hear through the grapevine that Major Vernon's not the manager there anymore.'

'That's right. He's retired. His nephew – Mr Ellroy – runs the place now.'

'His *nephew!* I should have guessed. It's like the Mafia in that place. Keep it in the family ... what's the word?'

'Nepotism,' I said (along with Seb and Anne).

'Look on the bright side, love,' Dad said to Mum. 'At least you don't have to sneak around the Rex anymore trying to avoid –'

'I never "tried to avoid" *anyone*! Much less "sneak around".'

Dad was about to say something else, but Mum cut him off.

'Coming face to face with Major Vernon never bothered *me*,' she said. 'When we used to take the children there I *always* held my head high. It's not *me* that did anything to be ashamed of.' Her eyes darted around the room and out to the hallway. 'Talking of being ashamed, where's Darryl? Isn't *he* going to say hello?'

Anne said, 'He's just popped out.'

'For what?'

'Wine.'

'But no one drinks. Do *you* drink, Seb?'

'Er ... no,' Seb said. 'Not really.'

'BAHM!' Liam threw a toy car.

'Don't do that, love,' Anne said.

'He's going to take someone's eye out one of these days,' Mum said.

'You said that the last time you were here, Mum.'

'And it's still true.'

'He doesn't throw them *at people*.'

'He shouldn't be throwing them *at all*.'

'Oh, this is nice,' Dad said, picking up the thrown car. He looked at his grandson. 'Where'd you get this, Liam, eh?'

It was the gold Cadillac.

'*You* must've given it to him!' Mum said.

'Not *this* one, love,' Dad said. 'Lesney's have only made one Cadillac. The Cadillac Deville. That was back in 1964, I believe. This is a Cadillac *Eldorado*. And no car we've *ever* made has been painted metallic gold.' He looked closer at the car. 'In fact ... this looks like real gold leaf. Lesney's have *never* used real gold leaf.'

Mum rolled her eyes. 'We're going to get the whole history of Lesney's toy cars now! Change the subject someone.'

Seb took a sideways step closer to me.

I can feel the warmth of his arm against mine.

Anne said, 'Dinner's nearly ready – Dom, help me in the kitchen, please.'

'You going to be okay here?' I asked Seb softly, indicating Mum and Dad.

He nodded and smiled. 'I'll try to stop Liam from blinding everyone.'

I want to unbutton Seb's shirt and lick his –

'DOM!'

'COMING!'

I went to the kitchen.

Anne was carving the roast.

She said, 'If Darryl doesn't come back, I will never forgive him.'

'Of *course* he'll come back.'

'I'm not so sure.'

'What do you mean?'

'Oh ... nothing. Get the Yorkshire puddings out of the oven, will you.'

Seb breezed into the kitchen. 'Your parents would like something to drink – Ooo, that roast beef smells delicious!'

'Thank you,' Anne said. She looked at me. 'Will you get drinks for – ?'

'I'll do it,' Seb said. 'Just tell me where everything is.'

I want to unbuckle his chinos and pull them down and –

Anne said, 'A bitter lemon for Mum. Lemonade for Dad. All in the fridge. Glasses over there. Thank you.'

'It's my pleasure.'

Seb set about pouring the drinks.

It's like he's been here a million times before.

The front door opened.

'Darryl,' I said, looking at Anne.

I heard his car keys clink on the console table.

'What does *he* have to drink?' Seb asked.

'Water,' Anne said, walking into the hallway.

I watched her whisper something in his ear, take two bottles of wine from him, and then shepherd him to the living room.

'So sorry I'm late, everyone!' Darryl said (as he had no doubt been instructed).

There were lots of 'hellos' and small talk about the heatwave, work, and last night's telly.

Seb stood behind me at the kitchen table, kissing my neck.

I pushed myself against him.

I could feel his erection.

'Would you like ... a Coke?' he asked, softly in my ear.

'Yes, please,' I said, rubbing myself against his crotch.

'And what would Anne like to drink?'

'Oh ... pour her a lemonade.'

He reached round me and poured the two drinks, grinding against me the whole time.

'I ... I might cum if I keep doing this,' he said.

'I ... might ... cum ... too.'

'Then I'd best stop!' He took a step back.

I turned to look at him.

I indicated the outline of his erection in his chinos. 'You still look pretty pleased to see me.'

He thrust his hand into his chinos and did some re-arranging. 'Better?'

'That depends on what we intend to do next.'

'I'm serving drinks to your parents.'

'Then it's *much* better.'

'Drink your Coke.' He cupped his hand round my cock bulge. 'It'll help cool you down. Shall I leave Anne's drink here?'

'Yeah. She'll be back in a second.'

He picked up the drinks and went to the living room.

I heard him say, 'Drinks for all!'

I sipped some Coke.

I've still got an erection.

Anne came back to the kitchen.

I held the chopping board in front of my groin.

'So far, so good.' She indicated the glass of lemonade. 'This for me?'

'Yeah,' I said.

'Your Seb is a wonder,' she said, sipping her drink. 'Everyone adores him.'

She called him 'my' Seb!

'Okay,' she went on, 'time to "plate up", as they say in posh restaurants. Let's do it quick. We don't want anything getting cold.'

Five minutes later we were announcing, 'DINNER'S READY!' and carrying the plates into the dining room.

We all sat round the table.

Seb was next to me, and he started rubbing his leg against mine.

I want to get under the table and suck his —

'Who wants wine?' Darryl asked.

'Not me,' Anne said.

'I'll stick with bitter lemon,' Mum said.

'I'll stick with lemonade, thank you, Darryl,' Dad said.

'I'm okay with Coke,' Seb and I said in unison.

We both laughed.

Darryl glared at us, mumbling something, and then poured himself a glass of wine (full to the brim).

'Where do you live, Seb?' Mum asked.

'Oasis Estate,' Seb said.

'Oh, they're *lovely* flats,' Mum said. 'We were offered a place there. Weren't we, Lionel?'

'We were, love,' Dad said.

'But my mum wasn't very well,' Mum went on, 'so we moved into Bradley Estate to be close to her. And Lionel wanted to be close to his sister – Didn't you, Lionel?'

'That's right,' Dad said.

'But then the two of them were dead within the year so . . .' She sipped some bitter lemon. 'It's awful to live in a place you don't like.'

'But *your* flat's like a palace, Mum,' Anne said.

'That's what *I* keep telling her,' Dad said.

'The flat *itself* might look like a palace, but the estate it's *on* certainly isn't. It was when we *first* moved in. Wasn't it, Lionel?'

'It was, love.'

'The concrete used to shine like marble. All the lawns were bright green and neatly cut. Everything was kept clean and tidy. People helped each other. But *now* . . . well, it's a graffiti-covered dump. And, of course, the lifts hardly ever work. So Lionel has to traipse up and down the stairs, and, with a heart like his, that's dicing with death on a daily basis.' She looked at Seb. 'He's had three heart attacks, you know. And a triple bypass operation.'

'I'm fine,' Dad said.

'You are *not* fine,' Mum said. 'And if you did have another heart attack on those stairs – who'd help you? Not any of the neighbours, that's for sure. They'd just walk right over you.'

'They're not *that* bad, Marian.'

'They are! There's absolutely *no* neighbourly spirit in the flats at all. None whatsoever. The people living next door don't even say hello, much less smile. That's rude in my book. Ignorant.'

'Perhaps they're thinking the same about you, Marian,' Darryl said.

'I *always* smile and say hello,' Mum said, glaring at him. '*My* mother taught me good manners. I would never, for example, sit with my elbows on the dinner table.'

Needless to say, Darryl's elbows were on the table.

He didn't remove them.

'Who wants more gravy?' Anne asked.

'I do, please,' Seb said.

'And me, please,' I said.

Seb's hand squeezed my thigh.

I want to suck him off under the table until he cums in my mouth and –

'MUM!'

Liam was struggling to get out of his high chair.

'Come on then, love,' Anne said, putting him on the floor. 'Go and play in the hallway.'

Liam started toddling out of the room.

Anne looked round the table. 'He can't sit still for too long.'

'He can't sit still *at all*!' Darryl said, downing his glass of wine, and pouring another.

'You need to have a lot of patience with children,' Dad said.

Mum said, 'You need to have a lot of patience with some *adults* too.' She glared at Darryl's elbows.

Seb said, 'My brother's going out with an old friend of yours, Anne.'

Oh, no. I haven't told him not to mention –

'Who's that?' Anne asked.

Don't say it! Don't say –

'Zoë,' Seb said.

Anne didn't flinch, but Darryl did.

'What a small world,' Anne said, flatly.

Darryl downed his wine and went to pour another.

'You've drunk enough, I think,' Anne said.

'Well, I *don't* think,' Darryl said.

'MUM!' Liam called from the hallway.

'Excuse me,' Anne said, getting up and going to the hallway.

Darryl looked at Seb. 'What's she been saying about me?'

'Who?' Seb asked.

'Zoë.'

'Nothing.'

Mum said, 'Why would Zoë say anything about *you*? *You* weren't her best friend.'

'I wasn't her *anything*,' Darryl said.

'Then she's a lucky girl.'

Seb squeezed my thigh again.

I want him to bend over the table so I can finger him and –

Anne came back to the dining room and sat down. 'Liam's just a bit restless.'

'It's all the excitement,' Dad said. 'Strangers in the house.'

'Well, if you came round here more often,' Darryl said, 'you wouldn't *be* strangers, would you.'

'He didn't mean *us*!' Mum said, glancing at Seb.

I squeezed Seb's thigh.

'It's nothing to do with *any* of that,' Anne said. 'Liam's just a bit . . . he's just got too much energy.'

'My brother's like that,' Seb said. 'Always has been. I've known him to get up in the middle of the night and go for a bike ride. I don't know how Zoë puts up with him.'

Stop saying her name!

Darryl was staring at his plate.

'MUM!' Liam called again.

Anne went to get up.

'Leave him!' Darryl said.

'I *can't* leave him!' She went to the hallway.

'If anyone wants to see a film at the Rex while I'm there,' Seb said, 'I can sneak you in for free.'

'That sounds like an offer we can't refuse,' Dad said. 'What's on at the moment, Seb?'

'Well, this week there's nothing special. But in a few weeks we've got *E.T.*'

'Oh, I've heard about that,' Dad said. 'It's about an alien monster that gets stranded on earth, right?'

'That's right, Lionel,' Seb said.

'I don't think it's a *monster* exactly,' I said.

'It's supposed to be brilliant.'

'It's more of a family film,' I said.

'I hear it's very good,' Dad said.

'It's directed by Steven Spielberg.'

'Oh, he did *Jaws*, didn't he?' Dad said.

'That's right,' Seb said.

'We all went to see that. Remember, son?

'I do, Dad. It was a brilliant night.'

'You liked *Jaws*, didn't you, Marian?'

'It scared me half to death!' Mum said.

'She was clutching my arm so tight!'

'I could barely look at the screen.'

Anne returned, 'Liam's fine – Did I hear someone mention *E.T.*?'

'It's on at the Rex next week,' Dad said.

'In a *few* weeks' time, Dad,' I said.

'Oh, I'd *love* to see that!' Anne said.

'So would I,' Dad said. 'Marian?'

'It's not scary, is it? Mum said.

'I don't think so,' Seb said.

'It's a *family* film, Mum.'

'Then we should see it as a family!' Dad said. 'Let's make a big family night out of it, eh?'

'I'd like that,' Anne said.

'So would I,' Mum said.

'And me,' I said.

Darryl started tapping his wine glass with a fork.

We all looked at him.

'Sorry to interrupt this heartwarming family scene,' Darryl said, 'but I want to make . . . a . . . speech.' He got to his feet.

'Oh, sit down, Darryl!' Anne hissed.

'Ladies and gentlemen,' Darryl went on, gazing round the table at us. 'There are two sides to every story. Am I right? Of *course* I'm right. The trouble is – in this family – only *one* side of the story ever gets heard. Do you know what side that is? I shall give you a hint. It's not mine!'

'You're making a fool of yourself,' Anne said.

'He's drunk,' Mum said.

'In fact,' Darryl went on, 'I don't have *any* story of my own as far as *you* lot are concerned. I am the storyless man.'

'You're the self-pitying man,' Mum said.

'Ignore him,' Anne said.

'That's right!' Darryl said. 'Ignore me! Just like you *always* do.'

'Should I go?' Seb said.

I grabbed his hand. 'No!'

'That's right!' Darryl said, looking at Seb. 'Stay! I want you to know *exactly* what kind of family you're about to get involved with.'

Dad said to Darryl, 'Why don't you go for a walk or something. Cool off. Come on!' He started to get up. 'I'll go with you.'

'I would *love* to go for a walk with you, Lionel,' Darryl said. 'But not right now. So sit down. Relax.'

Dad settled in his chair again.

We all watched as Darryl took a few gulps of wine.

Seb held my hand.

'*First*,' Darryl said, wiping his lips. 'I hope you all enjoyed the roast dinner you've been eating. The roast paid for with *my* money.'

'Don't say anything you'll regret, Darryl,' Dad said.

'The roast dinner,' Darryl went on, 'being eaten in the house I paid for. And how many thanks do I get? I'll give you a clue. It's somewhere between none and . . . zero!'

'Let's go!' Mum said, tapping Dad's arm and preparing to stand.

'No, no! You stay where you are, Marian. There's dessert still to come. And you wouldn't want to miss that.' He took a swig direct from the wine bottle. 'I could've had my pick of any girl in East London, you know. They were all after me. When I walked out of school, there would be a crowd of girls waiting outside. Everyone said I had the body of a matador.'

'And the brains of a bull,' Mum said.

'I could've been on the cover of *Vogue*!'

'Oh, not this old chestnut,' Anne said.

'You!' Darryl pointed at Anne. 'I gave it all up for *you*.'

Mum said, 'You had nothing *to* give up! You barely had a job.'

'I was working on my uncle's stall.'

'Part time!'

'It *wasn't* part time.'

'It was three days a week!'

'It was *six*!'

'He *paid* you for six, but you *worked* three!'

'My uncle loved me!'

'He felt *sorry* for you.'

'I wish he would move back here . . . I miss him . . . I miss him . . .' Tears started trickling down his face.

Mum said, 'There's three types of drunk. The jolly kind. The sentimental kind. And the nasty kind. And you are *not* the jolly kind.'

'Why don't you just shut up, you old bag!' Darryl said.

Anne and I got to our feet.

I said, '*You* better shut up, Darryl.'

Anne said, 'Yes. Be quiet!'

'Go for a walk!' Dad said. '*Now!*'

'I *will*, Lionel,' Darryl said, staggering away from the table. 'But without you, I'm afraid. Hope you're not offended. And shall I tell you where the walk will take me? To a place where someone listens to me. And when I say "someone" I mean . . . someone *special*.'

Darryl was at the living room door now.

'Wh-what're you saying, Darryl?' Anne said.

Darryl looked at her and grinned.

'He's seeing another woman,' Mum said. 'I *knew* it!'

'Darryl?' Anne said.

Darryl's grin got wider.

'Oh, just go if you're going!' Mum said. 'What're you bloody waiting for?!'

Darryl stepped into the hallway.

He took the car keys from the console table.

Seb said to me, 'He's too drunk to drive, Dom.'

'Oh, let him bloody kill himself!' Mum said.

'It's him killing someone *else* I'm worried about,' I said.

'Darryl?' Anne had stepped away from the table and was heading for the hallway. 'Darryl?'

I went with her.

'You can't bloody drive, Darryl,' I said.

'How long has it been going on?' Anne asked.

Mum said, '*I'll* tell you how long. He never stopped. From the day he met you. There was *always* another woman. I warned you. I *warned* you.'

Darryl started opening the front door.

I rushed to him. 'No!' I pushed the door shut. 'You've drunk too much. Give me the car keys, Darryl.'

'Fuck off!' Darryl pushed me away.

'Give them to me!' I wrestled with him to get the keys.

Seb rushed to help.

Liam started crying.

Mum rushed to comfort him.

'Shush, shush, darling,' Mum said, kneeling. 'The stupid man is just leaving and then everything will be all right.'

'Who *is* she, Darryl?' Anne said.

Seb and I struggled with Darryl.

A vase was knocked off the console table.

Liam started screaming.

'Oh, fuck it!' Darryl said. '*Keep* the fucking car!'

He hurled the keys.

They hit Anne's shoulder.

'How *dare* you!' Mum said, glaring at Darryl. 'Get out!' She stood up and rushed at him. 'GET OUT!' She

took off a stiletto and started hitting him with it. 'GET
OUT! GET OUT! *GET OUT!*'

Darryl cowered under her blows.

Mum hit him and pushed him until he was through
the front door.

Darryl staggered away from the house.

'AND DON'T *EVER* COME BACK!' Mum slammed
the door behind him.

We all stood in silence, staring at Mum.

Even Liam had stopped making a sound.

I looked at Seb.

He mouthed, 'Wow!'

Mum put her stiletto back on

She went to Anne. 'Are you okay, love?'

'Yeah, yeah,' Anne said.

Liam started crying.

Anne picked Liam up. 'What a lot of silly noise and
fuss, eh, love? No wonder you're crying! Right, Mum?'

'Absolutely.' Mum said. 'It's enough to make *anyone*
cry,' She held Liam's hand. 'But it's all over now. We're
all calm. And we all love each other. And the person we
love most is . . . *you!*' She kissed him. 'Do *you* love *us,*
Liam?'

Liam had stopped crying. He nodded.

Mum looked at Anne. 'What's for dessert, love?'

'Sherry trifle.'

'I *adore* sherry trifle. I'll start clearing the table.' Mum
went back into the living room. 'LIONEL!?'

We rushed in after her.

Dad was slumped in his chair.

He was gasping for breath and sweating.

Seb said, 'I'll call an ambulance.'

CHAPTER TWENTY-FOUR

Mum travelled to the hospital with Dad in the ambulance. The rest of us followed in a mini cab.

By the time we got there Dad was already hooked up to various machines and surrounded by medical staff.

Anne kissed Dad and said, 'I love you.'

I should do that.

But I didn't.

I went to the corridor outside.

Seb sat next to me.

He asked, 'Do you want me to stay or shall I – ?'

'Stay!' I said, grabbing his arm.

CHAPTER TWENTY-FIVE

An hour later.

'Do you want something to drink?' Seb asked.

'No, thanks. I'm fine,' I said.

Anne came out of the ward, holding Liam.

'They say he's stable,' she said.

'That's good, right?' Seb asked.

'I guess so, yes – Ooo, you're getting heavy, Liam.' She put him down. 'I'd best be getting back. Mum needs someone with her. Are you staying out here, Dom?'

'Yes,' I said.

'Keep an eye on Liam for me?' She kissed the top of Liam's head. 'Now you stay here with Uncle Dom and Uncle Seb, eh? Will you do that for me?'

Liam nodded.

Anne went back into the ward.

'What's that you're playing with, buddy?' Seb said to Liam, getting on his knees. 'A car! Shall we play with it together?'

Liam nodded.

'Come on, then. Push it to me!'

Liam pushed it to him,

Seb pushed it back.

Liam pushed it to him,

Seb pushed it back.

Liam pushed it to him,

Seb pushed it back.

Liam pushed it to him,

Seb pushed it back.

CHAPTER TWENTY-SIX

Thirty minutes later.

Liam said, 'Drink!'

'You're thirsty, buddy, eh?' Seb said. 'What do you fancy? A Coke?'

Liam nodded.

Seb touched my hand. 'Do you want anything?'

'Oh . . . I'll have a Coke too,' I said.

'I think I spotted a vending machine on the ground floor. I'll see what that has to offer.'

He started to walk away.

Liam rushed after him.

'Shall I take him with me?' Seb asked.

'Yeah,' I said. 'And see if you can get him something to eat. A sandwich or something. Who knows how long we're going to be here.'

CHAPTER TWENTY-SEVEN

Five minutes later.

Anne came back out of the ward.

'Where's Liam?' she asked.

'Seb's taken him to get something to drink,' I said. 'And hopefully a bite to eat.'

'Seb's so good with him.'

'Yeah.'

Anne sat next to me.

We sat in silence.

I asked, 'You okay?'

'Not really,' she said. 'You?'

'I . . . I don't know.'

People walked past us.

We sat in silence.

People walked past us.

We sat in silence.

Anne said, 'It was Zoë's idea to go to Southend that day. "It's such wonderful weather," she said. "Let's have a bit of fun before the exams start." So we went. We bought a couple of ice creams and sat on the beach. I noticed some young men nearby. They were playing with a Frisbee. One of them was wearing a bright red swimming costume. It was very tight. He saw me looking at him. I looked away. And then . . . then he threw the Frisbee and it was wildly off course. It knocked the ice cream out of my hand. He rushed over and apologized.

He offered to buy me another one. He asked me what flavour I wanted. I said I wasn't sure. He said, "Why don't you come with me so you can choose?" So I did. As we ... as we walked along the seafront ... I couldn't stop looking at him. His broad shoulders. His narrow waist. The muscles in his stomach. I can't remember what ice cream I chose. All I can remember is ... Darryl's gorgeous body, and how I'd rather be licking that. By the time I got back to Zoë I was in love. I told Zoë. She said, "You're not in love, you're in lust." And she was right. What I felt for Darryl was so ... so bright ... so dazzling. Like looking at the sun. It completely blinded me to what ... to what Darryl was *really* like. No, that's wrong. It didn't blind me *completely*. I did have *some* glimpses. But I deliberately avoided looking at them. So when people warned me about Darryl – when they told me he was no good for me – I got angry because ... for me to acknowledge that meant ... it meant I might lose him. Lose having sex with him. And I couldn't live if I lost that. I could live with losing everything else, but not that. And ... I *did* lose everything else. My relationship with Mum. My education. My career. My best friend. And by the time I let myself – *allowed* myself – to fully see Darryl for what he was – when I'd stopped fancying him – it was too late. The blazing sun had turned to a black hole and ... and I'd been sucked into it. And I was too proud – too bloody stubborn – to admit I'd ever been wrong. How could I admit it after ... after throwing so much away? Did I know for *sure* Darryl had always been seeing other women? For most of the time it fluctuated between yes and then no. But as time went on – especially with the "overnight deliveries" becoming more and more frequent – it became yes, yes, yes.' Anne looked at me. 'All that palaver at dinner about buying some wine. It wasn't about wine at all. It was about Darryl getting out of the house so he could phone whoever the current . . . "other woman" is.'

'What will you do now?'

'*Right* now? I'm going back to Dad's bedside. Beyond that . . . I'll have to make it up as I go along.'

CHAPTER TWENTY-EIGHT

I walk to the end of the corridor.
I walk back.
I walk to the end of the corridor.
I walk back.
I walk to the end of the corridor.
I walk back.
I walk to the end of the corridor.
I walk back.
I walk to the end of the corridor.
I walk back.

CHAPTER TWENTY-NINE

I walk to the end of the corridor –
And then I carry on walking.
Down another corridor.
Down another corridor.
Down another –
'Excuse me . . . is it Dominic?'
A man was standing nearby.
I said, 'Yes?'
'You probably don't remember me. It's quite a few years since we last saw each other. When you and your parents came to see *The Spy Who Loved Me*, I believe.'
And then I realized who it was.
'Major Vernon!' I said. 'Of *course* I remember you. Hello.'
We shook hands.
He'd lost some of his hair, but he was still dapperly dressed, and still had that matinée idol smile.
'I wasn't sure if it was you,' he said. 'You've grown up so much. But I thought there can't be many lads in the East End with hair your colour. Such a glorious shade of red. Like Rita Hayworth. I'm jealous.' He touched his thinning pate. 'Are you visiting someone here, Dominic? Not your dear mother, I hope.'
'No, no. My dad.'
'Oh, yes! He has heart problems! Is that right?'
I nodded. 'He's just had another heart attack.'

'What awfully rotten luck. But I'm sure he'll be fine. They can do amazing things these days.'

'. . . Why are *you* here, Major?'

'My nephew – my successor at the Rex – fell asleep on the roof of the cinema whilst sunbathing. Blisters galore. The doctors are currently deciding if he's to stay the night.' Major Vernon stared at me for a moment. 'You're growing so much like your mother.'

'It's the hair.'

'No . . . it's more than that,' he said slowly, as if trying to work out what that "more" actually was. And then he seemed to give up and said, 'Your mother's by your father's side, I have no doubt.'

'Yes,' I said.

'A remarkable woman. Two children and a poorly husband. It couldn't have been easy for her.'

'I guess not, no.'

'We used to be great friends, you know.'

'Really?!'

'Oh, yes. This was before she got engaged to your father. Her own mother – her name was Harriet, if memory serves – was very ill. Leukaemia. Your mother spent most of her time either looking after her or working at the cinema. Little time to have a social life. Or, indeed, any life at all. So my wife, Thora, and I used to ask her round for dinner now and again. Thora liked your mother very much. They enjoyed reading books together. Their own little reading group, you might say. My wife was a big fan of Patricia Highsmith. I remember her and your mother having passionate discussions about her novel *Carol*. And, of course, there was the poetry.'

'They read poetry together?'

'No, no, they *wrote* it.'

'My Mum . . . wrote *poetry*?'

'Didn't you know?'

'No.'

'Well, that does surprise me. She wrote some excellent verse. I always thought she would have a volume published one day. My wife thought so too. She found your mother the most talented young companion she'd ever met. That's why Thora was so upset when your mother . . . how shall I say? Withdrew from our social sphere.'

'Because of the film premiere thing?'

'The . . . "film premiere thing"?'

'*Doctor in the Slums*. Mum got a message through to the producer. *That's* why the premiere happened at the Rex. Then *you* claimed *all* the glory.'

It came out much blunter than I might have liked.

Major Vernon gazed at me a moment. 'Goodness,' he said, softly. 'That's the first time I've heard that . . . I had no idea your mother . . . Goodness, goodness. She never said *anything* to me about . . . Not a word.'

'But she *did* ask someone working on the crew to – '

'Yes, yes, I seem to remember something about that. But, honestly, that is *not* why the premiere happened at the Rex.' He shook his head again. 'Goodness. I have always thought your mother stopped visiting my wife and me – and stopped working at the Rex – because she met your father and . . . oh, I don't know. Perhaps there was some jealousy there. On your father's part. Towards her friendship with me and Thora.' He shook his head. 'I never realized . . . Never . . . '

'So how *did* the Rex get the premiere?'

'Oh . . . perhaps now's not the time to – '

'Tell me, Major. *Please*.'

'. . . Very well.' He took a deep breath. 'The Rex got

the premiere because I went to a dinner party one night and met Mr Dirk Bogarde. Do you want even *more* clarification?'

I nodded.

'A friend of mine – an aspiring actor – met a man, a theatrical producer – I forget his name – at some casting session, and this man said, "I'm having a dinner party at my flat in Mayfair. *Do* come along. You can bring a friend." *I* was that friend. It was a very swish affair. Lots of familiar faces from the world of theatre and film. One of them – indeed the person I was seated next to at the table – was Mr Dirk Bogarde. He looked as debonair and chilly as he always does. We started talking. And, as we talked, he grew more debonair and less chilly. Until, by the time dessert was being served – a peach melba, utterly delicious – Dirk was all debonair with no chill at all. He asked me to go back to his hotel with him. I said I'd have to phone my wife first and inform her I'd be late. Dirk said, "Tell her you won't be getting home till tomorrow. Possibly longer." And he was right. I finally got back to Thora three days later. She asked if I'd had a good time. She didn't mind what I got up to, she still doesn't, so long as I come back to her. And I told her I had an absolutely wonderful time. And, what's more, the Rex would be hosting the premiere of the new Dirk Bogarde film, *Doctor in the Slums*.'

A nurse came out of a nearby ward. 'Major?'

'Yes?' Major Vernon said.

'Your nephew's ready to go home.'

'Thank you, nurse.' He looked at me. 'I hope your father has similar "going home" news very soon.' He shook my hand. 'Good evening, Dominic. It's been wonderful to see you again.'

CHAPTER THIRTY

My dad died.

CHAPTER THIRTY-ONE

When I got back from talking to Major Vernon I saw Anne talking to Seb at the end of the corridor.

Seb was holding a Coke and a sandwich.

Liam was on the floor, holding a Coke and a sandwich.

Anne was crying.

And I knew.

CHAPTER THIRTY-TWO

Dad's dead.

CHAPTER THIRTY-THREE

'Do you want to see him?' Anne asked.

'No,' I said.

'Mum would want you to.'

'Not now, Anne . . . I . . . I can't. I can't.'

Seb was holding my hand.

'Okay, okay,' Anne said.

Seb squeezed my hand tighter.

Anne started to cry again.

Why can't I cry like that?

CHAPTER THIRTY-FOUR

Seb and I sat in the corridor.

Liam was asleep beside us.

Anne had rejoined Mum.

I said, 'I don't feel like anything's happened. I expected everything to feel different. But it doesn't.'

CHAPTER THIRTY-FIVE

Anne said, 'I'm staying with Mum tonight. She can't go back to her flat alone. Do you want to come with us?'

'No,' I said.

'You shouldn't be alone either, Dom.'

Seb said, 'I'll stay with him.'

'Thank you, Seb,' said Anne.

I asked, 'How's Mum?'

'She's still holding Dad's hand.'

'I *do* want to see her . . . see Dad . . . but . . .'

'It's fine, it's fine,' Anne said, hugging me. 'Mum understands. We all do. You should go now.'

CHAPTER THIRTY-SIX

I left the hospital with Seb.

He asked, 'Shall I get us a taxi?'

'I want to walk,' I said. 'Is that okay?'

'Sure. Whatever you want.'

We walked down Whitechapel Road.

Dad's been dead for two hours.

The sun was setting.

I said, 'It's getting dark.'

And then I chuckled.

'What?' Seb said.

'If you heard that line in a film you'd cringe, wouldn't you? Someone's dad has just died in hospital. That someone leaves the hospital and says, "It's getting dark." '

Seb laughed. 'That's nothing. I was about to point at those clouds over there and say, "There's a storm coming." '

'Oh, that's *much* worse!'

'Much worse!'

'Much, *much*, worse!'

CHAPTER THIRTY-SEVEN

By the time we were approaching Bow the whole sky was heavy with clouds.

Dad's been dead nearly four hours.

I pushed Seb into a doorway and kissed him.

I started feeling between his legs.

'Not here,' Seb said. 'Let's get back.'

CHAPTER THIRTY-EIGHT

It started to rain.

'It's warm!' I said. 'The rain's warm!'

Dad's been dead for four hours and twenty minutes.

Lightning.

Seb said, 'One . . . two . . . three . . . four . . . five . . . six . . . seven . . . eight – '

Thunder.

'The eye of the storm's eight miles away.' he said. 'Hard to believe the rain can get any worse.'

'Any *better* you mean!' I flung my arms wide, looked up, and started spinning and spinning. 'Come on!'

Seb started spinning with me.

The rain drenched us both.

I took my shirt off and threw it aside.

Seb took his shirt off and threw it aside.

We laughed and spun, splashing in puddles.

'LET'S RUN!' I shouted. 'COME ON! *RUN!*'

CHAPTER THIRTY-NINE

We ran and we splashed.
We ran and we splashed.
We ran and we splashed.

CHAPTER FORTY

As Seb and I turned into my street, we put our arms round each other's shoulders, staggering down the tarmac like two drunks, the rain lashing us, bubbling at our mouths and nostrils.

I kissed Seb's neck.

He turned to face me and –

We kissed deep, our tongues fencing.

I caught a glimpse of Billy over Seb's shoulder.

He was standing at his upstairs window.

He was holding a candelabrum, watching.

Look at us, Billy! Half-naked in the rain!

See how happy I am!

Without you!

We went to my front door and, as I fumbled for the keys, Seb rubbed his hands over the slippery expanse of my back.

I opened the door –

A letter on the doormat!

It was from Billy!

He didn't leave it in the garden because of the rain.

I kicked it under the console table before Seb had a chance to see it.

Seb wrapped his arms around me.

We groped at belt buckles.

'Upstairs!' I said.

We rushed to my bedroom.

I had left the window open.

The storm had blown my stories, drawings (and most of the pens and pencils) off the desk.

Rain was coming in.

Seb and I ignored it, trampling over the strewn stationery to tumble onto my bed.

Lightning!

Seb kissed me so hard our teeth clashed.

I ran my hand down the sleek firmness of his stomach and unbuckled his chinos.

Thunder!

Seb thrust against me, moaning.

I slipped my hand into Seb's boxers.

I grabbed his cock and started rubbing.

I felt his body convulse and –

'I . . . I'm cumming!' Seb gasped.

My hand became wet with Seb's spunk.

I felt his muscles unlock, his hardness break.

I withdrew my hand from his underwear.

I became aware of rain from the window hitting my face, the dampness of the pillow, my arm twisted at an uncomfortable angle.

'I . . . I'm sorry,' Seb said. 'I got a bit too excited.'

'What're you apologizing for,' I said, licking his cum from my fingers. 'It was sexy as hell.'

'Do you want me to wank you off?'

'No, no, let's save it.'

'You sure?'

'Yeah. We've got all night.' I got up and closed the window. 'And I should tidy up the room a little.'

'It's like a tornado's been through!'

'*We're* the tornado.'

'Good title for a song.' Seb felt between his legs. 'I'm a bit of a sticky-cum tornado at the moment. Can I use your bathroom?'

'It's down the hall.'

Seb left the room.

I waited till I heard the tap running, and then I rushed downstairs to get Billy's letter.

I will not *read it now.*

I might not ever *read it.*

I will throw it away.

I will burn it.

I will –

CHAPTER FORTY-ONE

Dear Dom,
We're coming to the end of our story. Don't you feel it?

Yes.

Where did we leave the last letter? Let me think . . . Oh, that's right! I'd just found out Trystan had used me to lure Theo back from the jungle. Goodness! What a cliffhanger! At least, I thought it was. But . . . did you think that? Have you been biting your fingernails in anticipation of what might happen next? Or have you been preoccupied with Seb and his sexy, white chinos. Although he's probably not wearing those sexy chinos now. Am I right? Is he lying beside you in a haze of post-coital bliss?

Not quite, no.

And, of course, there are other things going on in your life. I saw the ambulance arrive. I'm assuming it was your dad they took away. He looked very ill. I assume he's not coming back.

I hate you, Billy.

If that's the case, then his death is — thematically speaking — very apt. There's a lot of death in the story ahead.

Are you ready?

Just bloody tell me!

I stood in the middle of Theo's bedsit.

Outside, snow was falling. The snowflakes turned green in the neon light.

I was looking at the photograph of Theo and Kalvin.

The two of them standing outside the record shop. So happy. So in love.

I heard Trystan say, 'We can run away together, Billy. You and me. I've got money saved up. I've been doing lots of overtime. We can get a place of our own. Come on! Let's do it! Before Theo gets back.' He grabbed my arm.

I tugged it away. 'Don't touch me! You've been playing with me from the very beginning! That's why you were at the Crocodile House in the first place, wasn't it? You were looking for someone to be a replacement Kalvin. And the first requirement? They had to be interested in crocodiles! How many times had you been to the zoo before I showed up, eh?'

'I . . . don't remember.'

'How <u>many</u>, Trystan?'

'A few!'

'Had you tried with anyone <u>before</u> me?'

'That I met at the zoo? No.'

'But you tried with people you met . . . elsewhere?'

'. . . Yes.'

'Where did you meet them?'

'What does it matter?'

'Tell me!'

'Punk rock gigs. Pubs. Anywhere I might find someone who had a bit of Kalvin's "look". But after I got to know them a

bit I realized although they might look like Kalvin on the
<u>outside</u>, they had nothing of Kalvin on the <u>inside</u>. So I decided
to change tactics. I'd find someone who had a touch of Kalvin
on the <u>inside</u> first. And what was the most important thing
they had to have? A love of crocodiles. That's why I started
to go to the Crocodile House. The first few times I went
there I didn't meet anyone who was remotely viable.'

Viable?!

'<u>Viable?!</u>'
  'Yes! And then . . . I saw you. And you were drawing
the crocodiles! Just like Kalvin would have done. And you
had Kalvin's build. And then I spoke to you and – You had
green eyes! Just like Kalvin. It was uncanny. But there was
something else. Something that separated you from everyone
else I'd try to chat up while looking for another Kalvin. <u>You</u>
fancied <u>me</u>. You <u>wanted</u> me. And I thought, <u>This</u> one's going to
be easy!'
  'You bastard!' I said.
  'Why? What did I do that was so wrong?'

He can't be serious!

  I said, 'You can't be serious, Trystan!'
  'I'm <u>perfectly</u> serious. Think about it. When we first met,
you didn't know who you were, and you had no idea how to
discover it. Right? . . . <u>Right?</u>'
  'Yeah but –'
  'You didn't like the way you looked, and had no idea know
how to change it. You wanted a relationship with another
man, and that had eluded you. Right? . . . <u>Right?</u>'

'Yes! Yes!'

'And who changed all that? Me! I gave you an identity. I gave you a "look". I gave you sex. I created you, Billy. And you were happy . . . Well, <u>weren't</u> you?'

'Okay. I was happy. But . . . why did I have to look like Kalvin before you loved me? And don't give me all that "I love the essence of you" bullshit again.'

"It's <u>not</u> bullshit!'

'It <u>is</u>! You only fell in love with me — <u>really</u> fell in love with me — <u>after</u> you'd changed me into Kalvin's double. And I know the exact moment it happened. It was after I'd had all the tattoos done and you asked me to take off my shirt, and you wanked while you looked at me. <u>That's</u> when you fell in love! But by then it was too late. Because you'd already sent photos of me to Theo. The photos you took when I first wore the Crocodile Jacket.'

'That's right.' It was Theo speaking!

Theo had appeared in the doorway, holding the bottle of champagne he'd gone out to get. There was snow on his quiff and shoulders. 'Trystan sent me photos of you <u>before</u> you'd had the tattoos done. But, as you were wearing the Crocodile Jacket, it hardly mattered.'

I hate him!

'I hate you!' I rushed at Theo. My fists were clenched. I wanted to hit him.

You should hit him!

But I didn't. I just collapsed on the floor, crying.

Oh, Billy.

And, as I cried, I heard Theo and Trystan talking about me. They talked as if I wasn't there. Trystan said that as he had been the one to find me, I belonged to him. Theo said that as he had travelled five thousand miles to come back and be with me, I belonged to him.

You didn't belong to either of them.

I know what you're thinking, Dom. I didn't belong to either of them. Why didn't I just walk out of the bedsit and leave them both?

Because you had nowhere else to go?

Because I wasn't sure if I could live without Theo.

You couldn't still be in love with him, Billy?!

I wasn't sure if it was still love I felt for him. In fact, I wasn't sure about anything. Except one thing —
'I want you to tell me about Kalvin,' I said to Theo. 'If you don't tell me I'm leaving and you'll never see me again.'
'No!' Theo and Trystan said in unison.
'Yes!' I said. 'You have until the morning, Theo. In the meantime . . .' I picked up a blanket from the bed. 'I'll sleep downstairs in the rehearsal room.'
'You can't!' Theo said.
'It's snowing!' Trystan said.
'You'll freeze!'
I said, 'You two are colder than snow.'

Good title for a song.

I went down the fire escape. I went into the rehearsal room. I huddled in front of the fire in the rehearsal room, waiting for Theo to come down and tell me about Kalvin.
I watched snow fall through the tiny window in the door.
I watched the snow . . . and waited . . .

You should just leave! Go!

And then, just as the sun was coming up — and I'd given up all hope of Theo telling me anything — an envelope was pushed under the rehearsal room door.

Theo's written you a letter!

As you've probably guessed, it was a letter from Theo. I'm enclosing it here for you to read.

'What're you looking at?' Seb asked.

CHAPTER FORTY-TWO

Seb had come back into the room, a towel wrapped round his waist.

'Oh ... it's nothing,' I said, putting the letter from Billy (and the one from Theo) on my bedside cabinet.

'You haven't done much tidying.' Seb said, treading carefully over the strewn pages. 'Come on. I'll help you.' He started picking up sheets of paper. 'Oh, this looks interesting! Old gothic style lettering?'

'It's a page from a fairy tale.'

'A fairy tale *you* made up?'

'Yeah. I wrote the first version of it ... oh, years ago. When I was fourteen. But recently ... well, I hand wrote it in that gothic style script. It's a sort of ... calligraphy artwork, I suppose.'

'It looks amazing.'

'It's not finished. I'm thinking of decorating some of the capital letters. And all around the border.'

'Like an illuminated manuscript?'

'Yeah. But a bit more ... graffiti style. You know? A spray paint effect.'

'A clash of the medieval and modern.'

'Exactly!'

Seb looked closer at the page. 'I was going to say, "You're lucky the ink on it hasn't run." But perhaps if you're giving it a touch of the urban, it wouldn't matter.'

'No, perhaps it wouldn't. And perhaps ... Yeah!

Perhaps I should *deliberately* make the ink run. Then decorate it with red rhinestones. And gold leaf!'

'You look *very* sexy when you're talking about your art.' He put the page from the fairy tale on the desk. 'I can't wait to see it when it's finished – Ooo, I've just trod on something!' He peeled a page from his foot. 'You need to get this dry before it turns to papier-mâché. And all the other stuff near the window.'

'Let's spread everything on the desk, Seb.' I wiped the surface dry with a T-shirt. 'The heat from the lamp will help.'

I want to read the letter Theo gave to Billy.

Seb was picking up some typewritten pages. 'Are you writing a novel?'

'No, no. Not yet anyway. I'm typing up the stories I've written about the family. I keep hoping it might turn into a novel but . . . well, nothing's happened yet.'

I kept glancing at Theo's letter as I picked up pages from the floor and put them on the desk –

Dear Billy,
    I guess you're wondering why I'm writing to you about Kalvin instead of simply telling you. I'm doing it because, if I told you the story to your face, I would notice your reactions, and I'd be tempted to change the story

I skipped a bit.

One day, while I was serving in the record shop, Theo came out of the back office and said, 'I've just booked a band into the rehearsal room tonight. They'll be here at six.'
    'What're they called?' I asked

'Crocodiles & Cadillacs.'

Lightning.
Seb said, 'One . . . two . . . three . . . four . . . five . . . six
. . . seven – '
Thunder.
'The eye of the storm's seven miles away,' I said.

At six o'clock, just as I was closing the shop, two guys came into the shop and announced they were the drummer and bass guitarist of Crocodiles & Cadillacs. I took them round to the side gate so they could drive their van into the courtyard behind the shop.

I asked for payment up front. They said their manager would deal with it . . . when he turns up.

I said, 'Well, I hope he turns up soon.'

'So do we,' the bassist said. 'He's our frontman too.'

'It's raining so hard I can't see anything outside.' Seb was looking through the window. 'It's like . . . we're the only things on the planet.'

I was in my room, checking my records were all in alphabetical order (by name of artist), when I heard Crocodiles & Cadillacs start to perform a song. A slow, rhythmic, acoustic guitar was soon joined by a pulse of bass . . . a shimmer of cymbal . . . and then someone started to sing.

> The sky will be a different sky
> The sun will shine like new.'

That song again!

It was the most beautiful voice I had ever heard.

> 'You'll see yourself,
> you'll hear yourself,
> and wonder, 'Is that me?''

I stepped onto the fire escape so I could hear the voice more clearly. And then - almost as if hypnotized - I started to walk down the steps, across the courtyard, and into the rehearsal room.

'There!' Seb said. 'Everything's cleared up!'

The main electric lights of the rehearsal room had been turned off, and a candelabrum had been lit. The flickering flames cast enough light for me to vaguely make out the drummer and the bass guitarist, but the singer - who had the candelabrum on the floor in front of him - was bathed in a brilliant golden glow.

I gasped at the sight of him! His bright green Mohican haircut. His jacket painted to resemble the skin of a crocodile. And his eyes, glinting emerald.

Seb started kissing me, gently, tenderly.

After about five or six songs, the singer told the band it was time for a break, and then he came over to me.

He said, 'Hello. I'm Kalvin Sparrow. You must be the person from the record shop I spoke to this afternoon.'

'No, that was Trystan, my brother. I'm Theo.'

'I need to pay you, Theo.' He took some money from his pocket. 'I'm glad you stayed to listen to the songs. Did you like what you heard?'

'Yes,' I said. 'And I liked what I <u>saw</u> too.'

'You mean this?' he said, touching his jacket. 'It's my Crocodile Jacket. I painted it myself.'

'It's amazing,' I said. 'But I didn't mean the jacket. I meant the person wearing it.'

Kalvin smiled and gazed at me. 'Well, I like what I'm looking at too.'

I started kissing Seb, gently, tenderly.

I watched Kalvin and his band rehearse for the rest of the evening. At eleven o'clock they finished and started to pack up. I helped them put their stuff into the back of the van. The drummer and bass guitarist said goodbye and drove off.

'You're so beautiful, Dom,' Seb said, softly.

'Aren't you going with them?' I asked Kalvin.

'I live in a different direction,' he said.

I pointed at the top of the fire escape, where the window to my room was still open, spilling light. 'Would you like to come up for a coffee or something, before you . . . go in your "different direction"?'

'<u>Before You Go in Your Different Direction</u>,' Kalvin said. 'Good title for a song.'

'You should write it.'

'Perhaps I will. After we've had that coffee . . . or something.'

'You're beautiful too, Seb,' I said, softly.

Kalvin and I walked up the fire escape.
'I love this green neon light,' he said. 'Where's it coming from?'
'The local cinema,' I said. 'It's called the Regal. You can see it from my window.'

Thunder.
Seb said. 'One ... two ... three ... four ... five ... six –'
Lightning.
'Six miles,' I said.

I took Kalvin up to my room. He looked out of the window at the Regal cinema across the street, with its front aglow with green neon.
'I feel at home in this light,' Kalvin said. 'I use green lighting when I do my gigs. Green is the spiritual colour of crocodiles.'

Seb and I – still kissing – got on the bed.

'Crocodiles, crocodiles, crocodiles,' I said, indicating Kalvin's jacket (which he had taken off and thrown on the bed), the tattoos on his arms, and his guitar propped against the bookshelf. 'Why?'

The towel around Seb's waist was getting loose.

'Crocodiles are the most magnificent creatures on the planet,' Kalvin said. 'They can live for well over a hundred years. You and me . . . we'll live and die, and the crocodiles that are alive now will probably still be here. They'll still be watching, safe in their hard skins. We should worship them. They're the only things <u>worth</u> worshipping. I've got a big tattoo of one on my back. Do you want to see it?'

I nodded.

Seb removed the towel from around his waist.

Kalvin took off his T-shirt and then turned round. 'What do you think?' he asked.

A tattoo of a crocodile ran down the length of his spine, its jaws were up by his neck, its tail disappearing behind the waistband of his jeans.

The green neon glistened on his body.

I said, 'It's . . . wonderful.'

'If I move . . . it comes alive. Watch!'

He flexed some muscles.

The crocodile appeared to crawl.

'Do you want to touch it?' Kalvin asked.

I unbuckled my jeans.

My hands ran up Kalvin's back, over his shoulders, and around his chest.

My cock had never got so hard, so quick.

Kalvin thrust himself back, grinding against my

Seb pulled my jeans and boxer shorts off.

The next morning I asked Kalvin if he wanted to move in with me. He said, 'Yes.'

We ran our fingers over each other's bodies.

I introduced Kalvin to Trystan. The two of them shook hands and seemed to like each other.

Our erections gently touched.

Time passed,

That night, Kalvin played me a record by his band. Crocodiles & Cadillacs.

The King got older.

I said to Kalvin, 'You paint, you sing, you write songs. How can you do so many different things?'
'Because they're not different things,' he said. 'At least not to me. For me . . . well, it's like when you're on a plane.'

**And the crocodile's skin
got more and more adorned
with sapphires and rubies
and diamonds and pearls
and amber and topaz and opal,
and its claws became
longer and sharper
and more and more
golden.**

'I've never been on a plane,' I said.

'Well, neither have I.' Kalvin said. 'But let's imagine, eh? You're in a plane above the clouds. You look out of the cabin window and you see lots of mountain peaks poking up through the clouds. What a fantastic range of mountains, you think. But then the plane flies <u>below</u> the clouds and you realize . . . it was just one mountain. One mountain with lots of different peaks.'

And the reputation of the jewel-incrusted crocodile started to spread.

Later, as Kalvin and I lay in bed listening to his record, I asked, 'Why "Cadillacs"?'

'Eh?'

'The name of your band. Crocodiles & Cadillacs. I get the "Crocodiles". But "Cadillacs"?'

It spread wider

'There's a photo of Elvis Presley from 1957. It's taken at the International Amphitheatre in Chicago. Elvis is wearing a very special suit. It's made of gold lamé. You know the one I mean?'

'Sure. It's famous.'

and wider

'<u>Very</u> famous. But what is less famous - in fact, what hardly anyone talks about now at all - is the fact that Elvis <u>arrived</u> at that concert in a gold Cadillac. A Cadillac Eldorado to be precise. I saw the photograph of Elvis getting out of that car on my thirteenth birthday. And, when I saw it, I ejaculated for the first time.'

and wider.

Thunder.
One ... two ... three ... four ... five –
Lightning.
Five.

Kalvin told me he wanted to paint something on a larger scale.
I said, 'You can paint the walls in the rehearsal room if you like.'

Royalty from other lands came to see the crocodile.

The next day Kalvin went to a local decorating shop and bought cans of spray paint.

I lay in the opposite direction to Seb and started to suck his cock.

And all the royalty from the other lands said, 'The crocodile is so beautiful. The crocodile is so powerful.'

Kalvin started painting the walls in the rehearsal room. He would be there all day sometimes. When I got home from work I'd cook something to eat and take it down to him. But I wasn't allowed <u>in</u> the rehearsal room. I had to leave the plate outside the door. Kalvin didn't want me to see what he was painting until he was ready.

I sucked Seb's cock. I tasted the salt and sweat of him.

But no one ever said, 'The King is so beautiful. The King is so powerful.'

One night Kalvin came up from the rehearsal room much later than usual. There were glittered flecks on his fingers and face. 'Gold leaf,' Kalvin explained. 'It sticks to everything - Look!'
He pulled down his jeans and boxer shorts.
His cock glistened with gold.
'How did it get <u>there</u>?' I asked.
'The crocodiles - they turn me on.'

Eventually, the King became jealous of the crocodile

Seb sucked my cock, his tongue flicking and teasing me, like my tongue was flicking and teasing him.

I licked the gold from Kalvin's

I spat on my fingers, and then worked them between Seb's legs, lubricating his anus with my saliva.

And then, one night, I heard Kalvin calling from outside the rehearsal room, 'THEO! . . . THEO! . . . THEO!'

'D'you want me to finger fuck you?' I asked Seb.
'Oh, yeah,' Seb said. 'Do it!'

I looked out of the window.
'YEAH, YEAH, I'M HERE!' I called down to Kalvin.
'I'M READY TO SHOW YOU!' he called back up.

Thunder.
One . . . two . . . three . . . four —
Lightning.
Four.

The King yelled at the crocodile, 'MORE BEAUTIFUL THAN ME, ARE YOU?! MORE POWERFUL THAN ME, ARE YOU?! WELL, YOU'RE NOT! AND I'LL PROVE IT!'

I started to push a finger inside Seb.

I rushed down the fire escape.
Kalvin was waiting for me at the bottom.
'Close your eyes,' he said. 'And don't open them till I tell you.'
He guided me into the rehearsal room.

The King started to walk up the steps of the tallest tower in the Castle.

'Open your eyes!' Kalvin said.

I opened them . . . and gasped.

I heard Seb gasp, his anus tightening round my finger, sucking at it.

The golden light from the candelabrum shimmered over crocodiles, crocodiles, crocodiles.

𝔗𝔥𝔢 𝔠𝔯𝔬𝔠𝔬𝔡𝔦𝔩𝔢 𝔴𝔞𝔱𝔠𝔥𝔢𝔡 𝔱𝔥𝔢 𝔎𝔦𝔫𝔤 𝔤𝔬 𝔲𝔭 𝔱𝔥𝔢 𝔰𝔱𝔢𝔭𝔰 𝔬𝔣 𝔱𝔥𝔢 𝔱𝔬𝔴𝔢𝔯.

Seb spat on his fingers, and then worked them between my legs, lubricating my anus with his saliva.

Crocodiles were twisting and writhing across three of the four walls, their claws gleaming gold, their eyes sparking with red rhinestones.

'Do you want *me* to finger fuck *you* now?' Seb asked.

'Look up,' Kalvin said.
I looked up . . . and gasped.

'Oh, yeah.' I said. 'Do it!'

The ceiling was a vertiginous swirl of crocodiles. It was like gazing into the eye of a saurian cyclone.

I gasped, and my anus tightened round Seb's finger, sucking at it.

Kalvin said, 'I think of it as my Sistine Chapel of Crocodiles. It's not quite finished yet. There's still one wall left to paint. You see? But I wanted you to take a look at what I'd done so far. What d'you think?'

'I think it's beautiful . . . and sexy.'

'I think it's beautiful and sexy too.'

And then the crocodile started following the King up the steps to the top of the tower.

Kalvin and I watched each other as, item by item, we removed our clothes. And then we ███████████

███████████████████████████████████

                                        crocodiles

watching ███████████████████████

███████████████ ████████████████████

███████████████████████████████████

███████████

Seb started to push a finger into me.

███████████████████████████████████

███████████████████████████████████

███████████████████████████████████

            crocodiles ████████████████

███████████████████████████████████

███████████████████████████████████

███████████████████████████████████

███████████████████████████████████

███████████████████

I sucked and fingered Seb

███████████████████████████████████

███████████████████████████████████

Seb sucked and fingered me.

𝔍t takes a long time
for a crocodile to climb up
three hundred and thirty-three steps.

Afterwards, Kalvin and I lay naked on the rehearsal room floor, our bodies speckled with gold and spunk, and looked up at the vortex of crocodiles.

𝔅ut, eventually, the crocodile
got to the top of the tower.

'I've got something for you,' said Kalvin, reaching out for his Crocodile Jacket. 'I've been waiting for the perfect moment, and this is it. The two of us covered with cum beneath the crocodiles.' He took something wrapped in green tissue paper from one of the jacket's pockets.

'What is it?' I asked.

'Open it and see.'

Lightning.
One ... two ... three –
Thunder.
Three.

It was a ring. It was gold, and in the shape of crocodile. The eyes were red gemstones.

'There's an inscription,' Kalvin said.

I looked on the inside of the ring.

'To My Only Love From Your Only Love.'

Kalvin said, 'I love you, Theo. You're the only one in the world I will <u>ever</u> love. If you feel the same about me, put the ring on.'

I put the ring on.

We kissed.

I pushed back onto Seb's finger, then thrust forward into his mouth.

'You have to finish your Sistine Chapel, Kalvin,' I said, during a gap in the kissing, and indicating the one unpainted wall.

'I will,' he said. 'I know what it should be.' Kiss. 'A jungle scene. There'll be some hummingbirds. Small as thimbles and glittering like jewels.' Kiss, kiss. 'And a lagoon. With bright pink water lilies. And in the middle of the lagoon - floating on the surface - the shape of a crocodile. Huge. The Crocodile God.'

'Oh, it sounds amazing!!'

'It sounds like heaven.'

'I can't wait to see it.'

'You'll have to wait,' Kalvin said. 'I really want to take a break from the painting.' Kiss, kiss, kiss. 'I've been having lots of ideas for some new songs. I want to rehearse them with the band.'

The crocodile followed the King into a bare room with a tiny window.

Seb pushed back onto my finger, then pushed forward into my mouth.

'You can rehearse here any time you like,' I said.
'I was hoping you'd say that.' Kalvin said. 'I'm sure these crocodiles will inspire us.' Kiss. 'I'd really like the band to do another gig soon. To try the new songs out.' Kiss. 'I'm not sure where. The last pub we performed at has closed.

Seb moved position, so he could lay alongside me, face to face.

'Why don't you check out the Regal?'
'The Regal?'
'The cinema with the green neon.' Kiss. 'It hires the auditorium out for gigs sometimes. The place used to be a music hall years ago. There's a stage in front of the screen. It's decorated with gold cherubs. I think you'll love it.'
'I think so too.' Kiss.
'I'll phone Mr Jarman. He's the manager. He comes into the shop. He's got a bit of a soft spot for me.' I grinned. 'Or should that be <u>hard</u> spot. I'll tell him we want to pop in and check out the space.'

As soon as the crocodile was inside the room

Seb grabbed my cock and started rubbing.

I phoned Mr Jarman and he said me and Kalvin could pop into the cinema anytime we liked.

I grabbed Seb's cock and started rubbing.

The next day we went to the Regal.

the King rushed outside and locked the door.

I told one of the ushers why we were there. The usher said, 'Mr Jarman's not here at the moment, but he said you might pop in. This way please.' The usher led us towards the auditorium, saying, 'I'm afraid there's a screening still in progress. Is that okay?'
Kalvin said, 'Oh, that's fine.'

Seb and I kissed and rubbed each other, kissed and rubbed each other, kissed and rubbed each other, kissed and –

Kalvin and I went into the auditorium. The film that was showing was a cartoon.
The usher said, 'It's a Disney film. Peter Pan.'

Thunder.
One . . . two –
Lightning.
Two.

The King yelled at the crocodile, 'You will stay locked in this room!'

There didn't seem to be many people watching <u>Peter Pan</u>. Just a few family clusters here and there. Kalvin asked if he could get closer to the stage. The usher said he could.

I watched Kalvin walk down the aisle.

'No one except me will ever see you again!'

Seb and I kissed deeper and rubbed faster.

'No one will ever think you are more beautiful and more powerful than me ever again!'

Kalvin was looking at the stage when, in the film, a crocodile appeared.

Every day the King walked up the steps of the tower to visit the crocodile.

Kalvin looked at the cartoon crocodile, and then started to back away from the screen. He started saying something, but I couldn't hear what it was.

Deeper and faster, deeper and faster –

Then, suddenly, Kalvin was yelling, 'THAT CROCO-
DILE IS AN INSULT! A TRAVESTY!' He pushed past
me and ran out of the auditorium.

Deeper, faster, deeper, faster –

I rushed after Kalvin.

**The King's Doctor said to the King,
'Your Majesty,
climbing up the tower every day
will soon exhaust you.
You're not getting any younger.'**

'Did you see that joke of a crocodile, Theo?' Kalvin
said, grabbing my arm. 'How could anyone do that? I
don't understand.'
Kalvin's face was flushed. His eyes were wide. He was
becoming breathless.

But if King didn't see the crocodile

I said, 'Calm down, Kalvin, calm down.'

Lightning.
One –
Thunder.
One.

Deeper faster deeper faster deep –

'CROCODILES ARE SACRED!' he yelled in the direction of the auditorium. 'THEY SHOULD BE WOR-SHIPPED!'

he started to feel

People were coming out of the auditorium now. Ushers appeared as if from nowhere.

I said to them, 'It's all right. He's just a little upset. I'll get him home.'

lost and alone

Deeperfasterdeeperfasterdeeperfast –

and wonder why he existed at all.

And then Kalvin collapsed.

Seb said, 'I'm going to cum.'

I knelt beside Kalvin. His face was covered with sweat. His lips were turning blue. There was a vein throbbing in his neck.

And then, after several years of visiting the crocodile, the King felt a pain in his chest.

Everyone in the cinema was watching.

I yelled, 'DON'T LOOK AT HIM! DON'T LOOK AT HIM! DON'T LOOK AT HIM!'

The Doctor examined the King.

I said, 'I'm going to cum too!'

An ambulance arrived. I travelled with Kalvin to the hospital.

The Doctor said, 'These visits to the crocodile are damaging your heart. You must stop them at once.'

Lightning and thunder.
The eye of the storm!

Kalvin died.

'I'm cumming!'
'I'm cumming!'

This is the story of how I was born.

I pumped spasm after spasm of spunk over Seb's hand, over his stomach, and over his chest.

A doctor told me that Kalvin had a genetic heart condition. He could have died at any time.

Seb pumped spasm after spasm of spunk over my hand, over my stomach, over my chest.

I said, 'But he didn't die at <u>any</u> time. He died <u>now</u>.'

The King said,
'I cannot stop seeing the crocodile!'

While I was still a heartbeat within the
shell - quivering like a tadpole in the pond
of my mother's belly - I listened to the
endless whisperings that vibrated down her
aching spine, as I dreamed serenely in my
bubble of blood.

Seb and I held each other, our spunk mixing, bonding
us, skin to skin, thought to thought.

The days following Kalvin's death were a very busy
time for me. I tried hard to track down Kalvin's family,
but he didn't seem to have any. And his fellow band
members had vanished.

The Doctor said,
'I will put it bluntly, your Majesty.
If you climb up those steps again
in order to see the crocodile
you will die.'

Seb and I kissed, gently, softly.

I took it upon myself to organise a cremation for
Kalvin.

I didn't know who or what I was. I had neither
purpose nor reason. My stomach was bloated
with the hopes of others.

I assumed - I think rightly - that Kalvin would rather be cremated than buried.

My **mind** was **smooth and white**; I had no dreams to bruise my sleep, and my eyes were closed tight against the throbbing silence.

𝕿𝖍𝖊 𝕶𝖎𝖓𝖌 𝖉𝖎𝖉𝖓'𝖙 𝖜𝖆𝖓𝖙 𝖙𝖔 𝖉𝖎𝖊. (𝕺𝖋 𝖈𝖔𝖚𝖗𝖘𝖊 𝖍𝖊 𝖉𝖎𝖉𝖓'𝖙).

The day I collected Kalvin's ashes from the under-taker's was the same day Trystan and I found out the record shop was closing down. To be honest, I wasn't surprised. Sales had been down for ages, and - with me taking time off to deal with Kalvin's affairs - they'd all but vanished.

𝕾𝖔 𝖙𝖍𝖊 𝕶𝖎𝖓𝖌 𝖔𝖗𝖉𝖊𝖗𝖊𝖉 𝖌𝖚𝖆𝖗𝖉𝖘 𝖙𝖔 𝖈𝖆𝖗𝖗𝖞 𝖍𝖎𝖒 𝖚𝖕 𝖙𝖍𝖊 𝖘𝖙𝖊𝖕𝖘.

Seb and I lay in each other's arms.

𝕭𝖚𝖙 𝖆𝖋𝖙𝖊𝖗 𝖇𝖊𝖎𝖓𝖌 𝖈𝖆𝖗𝖗𝖎𝖊𝖉 𝖚𝖕 𝖔𝖓𝖑𝖞 𝖙𝖍𝖎𝖗𝖙𝖞-𝖙𝖍𝖗𝖊𝖊 𝖘𝖙𝖊𝖕𝖘 𝖙𝖍𝖊 𝕶𝖎𝖓𝖌 𝖋𝖊𝖑𝖙 𝖆 𝖕𝖆𝖎𝖓 𝖎𝖓 𝖍𝖎𝖘 𝖈𝖍𝖊𝖘𝖙 𝖆𝖓𝖉 𝖍𝖆𝖉 𝖙𝖔 𝖇𝖊 𝖈𝖆𝖗𝖗𝖎𝖊𝖉 𝖇𝖆𝖈𝖐 𝖉𝖔𝖜𝖓 𝖆𝖌𝖆𝖎𝖓.

Mr Meek told me and Trystan that we could keep our rooms above the shop (partly out of good will, but mainly so our presence would deter potential squatters), but, of course, we wouldn't be able to afford the rent - or much of anything else - unless we found somewhere else to work.

Seb and I breathed slowly, in unison, calm.

**The Doctor said, 'Once again,
I will put it bluntly, your Majesty.
If you try to get up those steps again
in any way you will die.
You must stop all attempts
to see the crocodile.'**

The voice of my mother came to me, distant
and muffled, like the purring of some gigantic
kitten, and I was aware of being both an end and
another start in a story outside of
myself.

I felt Seb's body relax and he fell asleep.

**The King said,
'But the crocodile has a hold over me.
So long as it is alive, I will try to see it.'**

I took it on myself to find Trystan and myself new
jobs. I went to see Mr Jarman at the Regal.

*Hang on! Theo wants to work at the place where Kalvin
died?!*

Mr Jarman offered me a job as usher. I said
I couldn't accept unless my brother worked at the
cinema too. So Mr Jarman offered Trystan a job as
usher too. Trystan asked if it was wise for me to work
at the place where Kalvin died.

It's not!

I told him I was over Kalvin's death.

That can't be true!

The Doctor said, 'Then there's only one solution, your Majesty.' The King nodded and said, 'The crocodile must die!'

I worked very hard at the cinema. Harder than I'd <u>ever</u> worked, in fact. I did all the overtime Mr Jarman offered. I covered for other people when they were sick. And I did it all with a smile on my face. But, of course - although I didn't fully realize it at the time - it was all an act.

Of course it was.

On the outside I cracking jokes, but on the inside I was cracking up. I was still grieving for Kalvin.

When the time was right, and I felt my mind twist and buckle with something like purpose, I pushed and squeezed myself into the world outside my dreaming pond.

The King sent a guard – armed with a spear – to kill the crocodile.

Things reached a head when the cinema's freezer

broke down. All the ice cream melted. Some of it spilled across the floor.

But the crocodile killed the guard.

I offered to clean it up. I <u>wanted</u> to clean it up. I filled a bucket with water and grabbed the mop. I started to sort out the mess. Only the mess would not be 'sorted'. The mop merely spread the ice cream over the linoleum. The more I mopped, the worse it became. I started to cry. And once I started . . . I couldn't stop.

Sounds like a nervous breakdown to me.

Mr Jarman took me into his office for a talk. He suggested I take some time off work, and seek 'professional help'. I took the time off work, but I didn't seek help. Instead, I curled up in bed and slept.

The King sent three guards – (armed with an axe, a crossbow and a spear) to kill the crocodile.

I stayed in bed and slept. For days. Weeks.

But – again – the crocodile killed the guards.

One night, after about a month of me sleeping most of the time, Trystan came into my room and said, 'Why don't you do some travelling, Theo? I've talked to Mr

Jarman about it. He said he would loan you the money.
You can go anywhere in the world.'

I was held in the air like a skinned rabbit,
blood dripping from my nose and fingers.

And that's when the idea came to me. I remem-
bered what Kalvin had said about the jungle he intended
to paint. He had referred to it as 'heaven'.

They put me in the arms of my mother and I
reached out and touched her, leaving a bloody
handprint across the swollen orb of her breast.

The first thing I needed to get was a passport. And
to get a passport I needed a photo of myself. I went
to a photo booth in a tube station to get them done.
But something must have been wrong with the machine
because no photos appeared.

These are the photos Billy found!

I spent all day trying to find a machine that worked.
Panic was setting in. But eventually I found one.

By now it was winter.

I decided I would travel to a jungle that, like Kalvin's
intended painting, had a lagoon. And I would scatter
Kalvin's ashes in the water. And then - perhaps - I
would be able to say goodbye to Kalvin.

Snow

I bought an old atlas from a second-hand bookshop. The Colombian jungle seemed to be the best place to go.

had started

I booked a flight to the airport closest to the jungle.

to fall.

I heard voices cooing my name, giving me identity in a strange, new planet.

I didn't know if was legal to take someone's ashes to another country, so I tucked Kalvin's ashes away at the bottom of my backpack and hoped - if it <u>was</u> illegal - I wouldn't be searched.

**The King said,
'Put a barrel of gunpowder
outside the crocodile's door.
Then blow the tower
and the crocodile
to smithereens.'**

I wasn't searched. The flight took nine hours. The landing was smooth.

My mother kissed the tender marshmallow of my skull and let her tears fall to my face.

I left the airport and hailed a taxi. I asked the driver if he knew a lagoon in the jungle that had crocodiles in it. He said he did. I asked him to take me there.

Hang on! It couldn't have been that simple!

I managed to rent a hut next to the lagoon.

Managed to . . . what?!

Five guards got a big barrel of gunpowder and carried it through a blizzard of snow to the tower, and then up the steps.

The hut was made of woven twigs and palm leaves. The area immediately around it was full of large flowers, with hummingbirds - small as acorns and glittering like jewels - drinking nectar from the multi-coloured blooms. Beyond that, of course, was the jungle.

The guards put the barrel of gunpowder outside the crocodile's room, and then they laid a thin trail of gunpowder down the three hundred and thirty-three steps to the bottom.

The lagoon in front of the hut was emerald green and flat as a mirror, with bright pink water lilies floating on the surface.

The trail of gunpowder was ignited.

The day after I arrived, I walked to the lagoon with Kalvin's ashes.

"A new beginning," Mum said.

I scattered Kalvin's ashes into the water. I
watched them float on the surface, then move out . . .
out . . . towards the middle of the lagoon.
   And that's when the Crocodile God appeared.

**The ignited trail of gunpowder sparkled
all the way up, up, up, up, up,
the three hundred and thirty-three steps.
And then . . .
an explosion!**

It was the biggest crocodile I had ever seen.
Bigger than any in the zoo. Three times as big. Its
eyes were blazing red.

**But only a tiny explosion,
because much of the gunpowder
had been made damp by the snow.**

The whole jungle became very still as the Crocodile
God opened its mouth and consumed Kalvin's ashes.
   And then, with a swish of its magnificent tail, and
a glimpse of its golden claws, it sank beneath the
surface of the water . . . and was gone.

**In fact,
the explosion was only powerful enough
to blow the door off the crocodile's room.**

I knew that - now I'd done what I came to do - I
should start thinking about leaving the jungle.

The crocodile walked out of the room

But the next day, when I looked out at the lagoon, I saw the Crocodile God there again. Its red eyes were looking at me.

and started making its way down the steps

And I knew what the Crocodile God wanted.

The guards tried to the stop the crocodile.

It wanted me to join Kalvin.

All of the guards – except one – were killed.

Every day - for how long? Weeks? Months? - I would sit at the edge of the lake.

The surviving guard rushed to the King and said, 'The crocodile has escaped!'

And every time I saw the Crocodile God, it was a struggle for me not to step into the water and swim out to it.

The King ordered everyone in the Castle to kill the crocodile.

I knew, of course, that my death would upset my dear brother, Trystan, that he'd be lost without me, and that I still had so much in this life that I wanted to do, and yet . . . what would be the point of doing <u>anything</u> without Kalvin by my side.

**And everyone in the castle
did try to kill the crocodile.
And everyone failed.
And lots of them
were killed or injured.**

One day, just as the sun was beginning to set, and the jungle was at its most beautiful, the Crocodile God appeared again and gazed at me with its brilliant, blood-red eyes.
I stepped into the lagoon.
The Crocodile God swam closer.
I took another step -

**The crocodile walked out of the Castle
and went to the nearby lake.
It cracked though the frozen surface
and disappeared beneath.**

And that's when the postman arrived.

The what *arrived?!*

**When the King heard what had happened
he rushed out of the Castle ~
barefoot in the snow ~
and went to the edge of the lake.**

The postman called out that he had a letter for me.

Theo's just playing games with you, Billy!

The King saw the hole in the ice that the crocodile had made.

I walked back out of the lagoon to get the letter from the postman.

None of this is real!

The King stood there for so long that icicles started to form on his nose and chin.

The letter was from Trystan.

The King caught a chill that night that turned to pneumonia. Many feared he would die.

He'd also sent some photographs of Kalvin . . . Wait!

But he didn't.

The photos were <u>not</u> of Kalvin. They were of someone who <u>looked</u> like Kalvin. Trystan said his name was Billy.

I know how this finishes.
I skipped the rest of Theo's letter.
I found the page where Billy started writing again.

I know what you're thinking, Dom. Theo's letter is just one lie after another.

Exactly!

A taxi ride into the jungle? A hut right by a lagoon? A postman arriving with a letter? It's all make-believe. A fantasy.

Obviously!

Theo clearly didn't take my distress at being manipulated into looking like Kalvin seriously.

He's not taking it seriously at all!

I decided then and there to leave Theo. And Trystan.

Good for you!

**When the King had fully
recovered from pneumonia
he went to the edge
of the lake again
and stared at the water.**

I was just about to walk out of the rehearsal room (for good!) when Theo and Trystan walked in.
They looked very calm, smug almost.

**The King still wanted
to see his beloved crocodile.**

'Have you read the letter?' Theo asked.
'Are you happy now?' Trystan asked.
'He doesn't <u>look</u> happy,' Theo said.
'He doesn't.'

'Why aren't you happy, Billy?'

'Because none of it is real!' I said.

'It might not be real,' Theo said, 'but, I assure you, it's all true.'

I said, 'Oh, you're such a pretentious wanker!'

That's what I called you, Billy.

'Me and Trystan have been talking,' Theo said, 'and we've we've come to an arrangement.'

'Arrangement'?!

In fact, every single day for the rest of his life the King went down to the lake hoping to catch a glimpse of the jewel-encrusted crocodile.

'Arrangement about what?' I asked.

'You,' said Trystan.

'Me?'

'We'll share you,' said Theo.

Share *you?!*

'<u>Share</u> me!?' I said.

Theo nodded. 'That's right. I'll have you weekdays.'

'And I'll have you weekends,' Trystan said.

The bastards!

On many, many occasions,

the King rushed into the lake,
crying, 'I'M COMING TO YOU,
MY BELOVED CROCODILE.
I'M COMING!'

'You bastards!' I said, 'How . . . how can you treat me like this? Like I'm just your . . . your toy. Your plaything.'

But Guards always managed
to swim out and bring the King
back to the castle.

'Oh, you <u>are</u> exaggerating,' Theo said. 'Isn't he, Trystan?'
'<u>Wildly</u> exaggerating, Theo,' Trystan said.

You're not, Billy!

'I'm <u>not</u>!' I said. 'It's unforgivable, what you've done. I don't know that much about Kalvin — only what you've told me — but even <u>I</u> know he wouldn't have treated <u>anyone</u> like this. He'd be angry with you. So would the crocodiles. <u>His</u> crocodiles!' I pointed at the paintings. 'They're angry at the way you've treated me! Aren't you, crocodiles? <u>Aren't you?</u> <u>AREN'T YOU?</u>'

And, no matter how many times
the King ran into the lake
calling for the crocodile
he never – ever! –
saw the crocodile again.

And that's when the painted crocodiles started to move.

WHAT?!

They started to twist and writhe out of the walls. They fell from the ceiling.

WHAT?!

Their golden claws scraped across the floor.

WHAT?!

Theo and Trystan backed towards the rehearsal room door.

The crocodiles started walking towards them, chomping their jaws.

'They're going to kill us!' Theo cried, looking at me. 'Stop them!'

'Stop them!' Trystan cried

'Certainly not!' I said, smiling. 'I'm having too much fun watching.'

Theo made a leap for the door. A crocodile's tail lashed out and slammed the door shut. Another crocodile bit into Theo's leg. He screamed, spraying blood. Another crocodile bit Trystan round the waist. Blood spurted over Trystan's white chinos. Another crocodile pulled Theo into the middle of the room. Other crocodiles started biting Theo's legs. His left leg was severed below the knee. Another crocodile bit Trystan's arm off above the elbow. Blood was spilling across the floor and –

Okay, okay, enough!
I stopped reading.

> '*I miss the way I told you stories,*
> *I miss the way you wanted more.*'

Billy had started to sing next door.

He knew I must have finished with the letters. He wanted me to go to him.

> '*I miss the way you took the Cadillac,*
> *And you loved the jacket that I wore.*'

And – oh, yes! – I *would* go to him. He'd been playing with me every bit as much as Theo and Trystan had played with him. And I wasn't going to let him get away with it.

> '*But the thing I miss the most –*
> *The thing I'd die to see again –*
> *Are the Crocodiles in Your Eyes.*

I checked that Seb was still asleep, and then I got out of bed.

I put on my jeans and shoes.

> '*Oh, just one more time, let me see*
> *The Crocodiles in Your Eyes.*'

Oh, you'll see them, Billy. And I hope they bite your fucking head off.

CHAPTER FORTY-THREE

The sun was rising now.

Billy's front door was ajar.

'Billy?' I pushed the door open.

The candelabrum – candles lit and flickering – was at the bottom of the stairs.

I stepped inside . . . and gasped.

There were crocodiles everywhere.

Crocodiles on the hallway walls, crocodiles on the hallway ceiling, crocodiles on the doors, crocodiles on the bannisters.

'It's finished, Dom,' I heard Billy say from above. 'Have a look round.'

I picked up the candelabrum.

I went into the front room.

All the windows had been painted, and the dazzling sunrise was giving them the effect of stained glass.

Crocodiles, crocodiles, crocodiles.

I looked in the back room.

Crocodiles, crocodiles.

And the kitchen.

Crocodiles.

'I know you're angry with me,' I heard Billy saying. 'You got to the end of my final letter and thought, "Billy's been playing with me all along. Everything he told me, everything he's written to me – it's all been lies!"'

I started walking up the stairs, lost in a world of candlelight and crocodiles.

'But you're wrong to think that,' Billy went on. 'I haven't been lying to you at all. All I've done is tell you something that's . . . *unreal*.'

I was at the top of the stairs.

Hummingbirds were beginning to appear in the paintings now, small as thimbles, glittering like jewels.

'Just like the paintings you're looking at now, Dom. They're not *real* hummingbirds. They're not *real* crocodiles. But tell me . . . can't you hear those tiny wings beating? Don't you feel the thrill of being close to so many crocodiles?'

You know I do, Billy.

I went into the upstairs front room.

On one of the walls, behind some foliage, a lagoon could be glimpsed, bright pink water lilies floating on the surface. In the middle of the lagoon was the largest crocodile of all, its eyes blood-red and glittering, its golden claws shimmering beneath the water.

It's the Crocodile God.

I gazed at it . . .

I gazed at it . . .

The sunlight – getting stronger by the second – was now blazing through the painted windows.

'You like what you're seeing, don't you, Dom?'

I do.

'And perhaps . . . you're not so angry with me anymore.'

Perhaps.

'And perhaps your anger is being replaced with something else. A memory. A memory of what it was like to see me for the first time. How much you once wanted me. Am I right?'

Yes.

'And how much . . . you want to see me again.'

I stepped into Billy's bedroom.

'Hello, Billy,' I said.

Billy was fully dressed (jacket and boots on), and holding the Crocodile Guitar.

All the furniture in the room had gone.

'Hello, Dom,' he said, smiling.

'Are you . . . are you leaving?'

'Yes. Everything I needed to do here . . . it's all done.' He took a step towards me. 'We've been on quite a journey, haven't we?'

'. . . Yeah.'

'And now you're on another journey. With Seb in the sexy, white chinos. Although, as I said in the letter, I doubt if he's wearing them, or much of anything, right now.'

'Did you hear us having sex?'

'Did you *want* me to hear you?'

'I don't care if you did or didn't.'

'Then I've picked the right time to disappear – But first!' He took a felt tip pen from his pocket. 'I'd like to leave you with something.' He went to draw on my neck.

I flinched back. 'Wh-what're you doing?'

'It'll be very small.'

'*What* will?'

'Let's call it a temporary tattoo, shall we? You said you were thinking of getting one. If you like this, you can have it done permanently.' His green eyes glittered. '*Please*, Dom.'

I stared at him a moment, and then I threw my head back, waiting for the pen's touch.

Billy started drawing on my neck, between the collar bone and jaw, the place you might leave a lovebite.

'How will I explain this to Seb?'

'Tell him you did it yourself.'

'I don't want to lie to him.'

'Of course you don't,' Billy said, grinning. 'But you will – There! All done!' He put the pen back in his pocket. 'Goodbye, Dom.'

'Goodbye, Billy.'

He walked out of the room.

I heard him go down the stairs.

I heard the front door open . . . then close.

He's gone!

The house was very silent.

Sunlight filled the room with a kaleidoscope of jewel-like, shimmering colours.

Did that crocodile move?

I walked out of the room and down the –

Is that crocodile moving?

Is that one?

That one?

I ran out of the house.

I could hear traffic and birdsong now.

Somewhere, a radio was playing.

I went back next door, and then up to the bathroom.

I stood in front of the bathroom cabinet, and looked at my refection.

At the 'tattoo' Billy had drawn on my neck.

It was Billy's tag.

His signature.

'DOM!'

Seb!

'I'm here, I'm here!' I called, rushing to the bedroom.
Seb was getting out of bed.

'I woke up and you were gone,' he said.

I sat on the edge of the mattress.

'Sorry,' I said. 'I just popped outside to ... to ...'
And suddenly I started to cry. It was so surprising – so
overwhelming – that I clutched hold of Seb, as if I were
sinking in quicksand. 'I'll never see him again.'

Seb held me. 'It's okay,' he said. 'Grief gets us like this.
I was the same when my Mum died.'

'I'll never see him again ... I'll never see him again ...'

Years passed,
and when the King
was on his deathbed,
he said, 'I want my body burnt
and my ashes scattered
onto the lake.'

The King's wishes were carried out.
(Of course they were.)
It was the middle of a heatwave,
and the lake was covered
with bright pink water lilies,
and there were hummingbirds,
small as thimbles, glittering like jewels.

As the King's ashes floated
to the centre of the lake
... the crocodile appeared.
Everyone now
referred to it as

The Crocodile God.
The Crocodile God's jewels
and golden claws
sparkled and dazzled
in the sunshine.

The Crocodile God
swallowed the King's ashes,
and then disappeared
below the surface again.

It is said that
the Crocodile God
still lives in that lake.
Seeing it is a good omen.
It means a life full of love.
I haven't seen the Crocodile God yet.
But I hope I will.
One day.

EPILOGUE

Dear Reader,

Well, here I am, your storyteller, Dominic, now writing to you in the form of a letter.

I suppose you're wondering why.

Well, there're a few reasons.

First, I felt like it.

Second, I thought (I *hoped*) it would be a surprise.

And third, the conversational tone would probably help me do all the 'wrapping up' stuff a bit quicker.

So here goes . . .

Dad's funeral service was, as you'd expect, like having my skin sandblasted away, and then walking through a vinegar shower (how's *that* for an overwrought simile?) Seb helped me get through it. A lot. But so did Mum and Anna, who were both at their best throughout. They organized everything. The two of them gave wonderful eulogies (and didn't press me when I said I didn't want to – wouldn't be *able* to – say anything). And they both looked immaculate in black.

A few weeks after the funeral, Mum moved into the remaining spare room in Anne's house. It made perfect sense: Mum didn't want to live alone (especially in a place where, as you know, she didn't want to live anyway), and she and Anne – now Darryl had gone – were back to being the best of friends again. (That's a bit of an over-simplification, but I'm sure you don't want anything any more detailed at this stage).

And what of Darryl? Well, (another over-simplification) he moved in with the woman he'd been seeing (we never found out who it was), left her after a few months for another woman, and then left her and moved to Spain to live with his Uncle Ernie. At which point we stopped hearing from him. I know it's easy to condemn and dismiss Darryl. But – to some extent – I can sort of see his side of the story. It couldn't have been easy being part of a family that clearly disliked him right from the start. And there's no doubt that when Darryl first met Anne he'd been just as blinded by lust as she was, and, once he'd got his sight back, he felt, just as Anne did, that he'd made a lot of wrong decisions and was now trapped in a life he no longer wanted. Of course a great deal of his behaviour was totally wrong and utterly disgraceful, although I hesitate to say unforgivable. And please, *please* believe me, I am *not* making excuses for him. All I'm trying to do is . . . understand. It's important, I think, to try to understand *any* story from *all* sides.

And what about the house, I hear you ask? Surely Darryl owned half of it? Yes, he did. But with the money Mum got from Dad's insurance, plus her and Dad's savings, she was able to pay Darryl off (and there was still enough left over to finish the decorating *and* get the garden tidied and re-turfed).

How did I feel about living with Mum again? Fine. She changed a lot after Dad died. She became more relaxed. She made new friends. She got a part-time job in the local library. And she loved being in close contact with her grandson (who, as Anne kept saying, was the only thing that made all the 'Darryl stuff' worthwhile). And, talking of Liam, he changed too. The tantrums stopped. The car throwing stopped. And he could listen to Mum telling stories for hours.

Mum's stories weren't fairy tales anymore. They were stories from Mum's past, some about Grandmother Harriet, some about working at the Rex, but, mostly, they were about my Dad. Sometimes I'd overhear her, and think, 'Oh, it didn't happen *that* way, Mum,' 'Oh, that didn't happen, Mum, *at all*,' or, but . . . well, it didn't matter. Because this unreal version of my dad's life felt . . . well, it somehow felt more truthful than what had actually happened. It made me wish I could go back in time and relive my life, and, equipped with this truth, get to know Dad all over again.

And now to answer the question you're all asking (at least I hope you are, otherwise I haven't written this whole thing properly): what happened to me and Seb? Did we stay as much in love as we were during that heatwave of 1982? Of course we didn't. It lasted until the end of my first term at St Martin's School of Art, and then Seb met someone else at the Queen Mary (the university where he would eventually get a first class degree), and I would've been heartbroken were it not for the fact that *I'd* already met someone else too, a guy who worked in the bookshop across the road from St Martin's. Seb and I stayed good friends, though, and I was his shoulder to cry on when his relationship with his fellow student disintegrated. But in hardly any time at all Seb had met someone (in a local pub), who I met once and liked a lot, but before I had a chance to meet them again, *they'd* gone off with someone else, and then I broke up from my bookseller because I'd met . . . oh, it sort of went on like this for quite a while. Life can be a lot messier and more confusing than a novel. Yes, even this one!

Well, we're just about at the end now. But there's one last thing I want to tell you about. It happened just after that morning when I'd said goodbye to Billy, and had gone back to the house and burst into tears.

Seb got dressed and made some breakfast, and we sat in the garden to eat it.

'I nearly forgot,' Seb said. 'I've got you a present.'

He reached in the back pocket of his chinos.

'What is it?' I asked.

'Open it and see.' He handed me something wrapped in green tissue paper. 'I'd meant to give it to you after we'd had dinner yesterday, but then . . .'

'The plot changed.'

'Yeah.'

Inside the tissue paper was a ring. It was gold, and in the shape of a crocodile. The eyes were red gemstones.

'I got it ages ago,' Seb said. 'In Yesterday's Treasure.'

'Your favourite shop!'

'That's right! I knew one day I'd find the right person to give the ring to. And now I have.

'Thank you,' I said. 'It's wonderful.'

'It's got an inscription on the inside.'

I read it but, of course, I knew what it would say:

To My Only Love From Your Only Love

'And you *are*,' Seb said. 'My only love. Always.'

'And you're mine,' I said. 'Always.'

We kissed.

'Look!' Seb said, pointing.

A rainbow, so vivid it looked spray-painted, arched across a clear blue sky.

Seb said, 'Now, if you put something like *this* in a novel – two lovers declare undying love, and then they look up and see a rainbow – no one would believe it, would they.'

I laughed. 'No. No one would believe it at all.'
Except *you*, I hope, dear Reader.

Yours Truly.

Dom

xxx

THE STORIES WE TELL

An Interview with Philip Ridley

Crocodilia is such a multi-layered, firework display of storytelling. Where on earth – *how* on earth – did you start writing it?

To be honest, it didn't start out being a 'firework display' at all. It started out very simple. This is going way back. When I was still at school.

You wrote it at school?!

Well, I started making notes for it when I was about seventeen. And then I wrote the first rough draft – very, very rough draft – during the summer after I'd left school, when I'd turned eighteen, and was waiting to go to Art College.

Like Dominic in the novel.

Oh, Dominic's basically me at that age. He's living with his parents in the East End of London. He's passionate about art and writing. He's gay. He's a bit of a loner. He's waiting to start studying at Art School. And he's also waiting for his – cliché alert! – 'life to begin.'

But you didn't move out of your parents' home and –

Have a fling with the sexy punk next door? No. Unfortunately. In fact, when I wrote that first draft I hadn't met anyone. So it was very much me imagining what having a relationship would be like.

You were literally writing about the 'man of your dreams'.

You could say that, yes.

And the rest of the plot?

In that initial draft it was extremely simple. Hardly a 'plot' at all. Dominic moves in with his older sister. He falls in love – or, at least, in lust – with Billy, who lives next door, and the two of them embark on a summer of sex and storytelling.

And the stories were . . . ?

Again, very simple. Billy tells Dominic about a previous lover, and Dominic tells Billy about his family. That's all.

So no letter writing? No stories within stories? No surprising twists, and sudden leaps into the uncanny?

None of that. The initial draft wasn't much more than a glorified short story really. But, as you can see, it sort of contained the DNA – or the armature, if you like – around which all the future drafts would evolve.

Can you say something about this 'evolution'?

Well, the novel became an ongoing project when I was at St Martin's.

That's the Art College you went to?

That's right. St Martin's School of Art in London. I took a degree in Painting. But I soon started working in lots of different media. I took photographs. I was making experimental videos. I was shooting short narrative films on Super 8. I was writing, of course. And, by the end of my second year, I had started experimenting with Performance Art pieces where I did long – very long – monologues. Most of them were autobiographical. Some were science fiction. Some were horror. Some were a mixture of all three. And ... oh, yes! Some were fairy tales.

And so you had Dominic write a fairy tale.

Exactly. That's sort of how the 'evolution' of the novel happened. I was constantly incorporating new things into the text. For example, in the first week of being at St Martin's I was shown – as a sort of new student ritual – the graffiti in the basement that had been done by the Sex Pistols.

They did their first-ever gig at St Martin's, didn't they?

In 1975, yes.

And so you had *Dominic* see that same graffiti in the novel.

That's right. Though, of course, Dominic sees it when he goes for his interview to get in, rather than actually being a student.

You weren't tempted to evolve the story into Dominic *being* at art school?

No, no. It was very important I kept it set in the summer before. That 'in-between' time. The hovering moment when he's eighteen and, as I said, 'waiting for his life to begin'. But as for the actual year the novel was set . . . well, yes, that did change. It kept up with the year I was working on it. Until I finally settled on keeping it at 1982.

Did the characters change?

Not so much Dominic, but Billy . . . oh, he changed a lot. Including the way he looked.

You mean he wasn't always a 'sexy punk'?

Well, he might have been sexy, but, no, he wasn't a punk. What happened was, I made good friends with someone in my year at St Martin's, and he was a punk. Ripped jeans, torn T-shirt, studded leather jacket, tattoos, and, yes, a Mohican haircut.

Green?

No. Blue-black. But it was still very striking. In fact, everything about him was striking. He was a bit of a college heartthrob.

For you too?

Oh, yes. But, to be honest, it was his painting that excited me the most. He was – he still is – a brilliant artist. And there were lots of similarities between his work and mine. We were both figurative. We both created images full of magic with a hint of menace. Sometimes more than a hint. And we both had a penchant for provocation. The two of us became very close. He had one of my images – called The Sleeping Moon *– tattooed on his arm.*

Very Billy Crow.

A lot about him was 'very Billy Crow'. Not just the way he looked, but his sexual allure. His charisma.

Did he paint crocodiles?

No, it was me who did that. Crocodiles have always fascinated me. And, at St Martin's, they soon became part of my own personal iconography.

Along with?

Oh . . . mountains, rainbows, chimneys, knives, ladybirds, Elvis, fossils, flamingoes, cockroaches, stars, glitter jackets, James Dean, butterflies, burnt trees, Cadillacs, roses, mirrors, harpoons, bullets, dolphins, and . . . oh, yes! Crows!

Hence Billy's surname.

That's right. The first piece of art I ever 'professionally' exhibited was a charcoal drawing called Corvus Cum. *It*

*was shown at the ICA in London in 1981. It was of a man ejac-
ulating a crow.*

That could almost be an image from the novel.

*Well, everything I was doing sort of fed into everything
else I was doing. The paintings. The photographs. The short
films. The Performance Art. And, of course, there were all
the artists whose work I was being introduced to for the first
time. Jean Cocteau, Louise Bourgeois, Joseph Cornell, Derek
Jarman, Frida Kahlo, Francis Bacon . . . oh, the list is endless.
And it was a* particularly *exciting time to be at Art College.
There was a huge buzz about graffiti art. Magazines were full
of photographs of the subways in New York. Some students
in my year started doing graffiti-style paintings. They painted
huge murals in the coffee bar. It was thrilling to be around. The
sheer energy of it.*

So that's why graffiti is mentioned in the novel?

*Yes. Although I've always seen the kind of artworks Billy
creates as having a . . . well, a more 'fine art' edge.*

**His work is described as the 'Sistine Chapel of
Crocodiles'.**

Exactly. Michelangelo with a dash of Keith Haring.

**Can you say something about the novel's first pub-
lication?**

Well, for most of the time I was at St Martin's Crocodilia
*was an ongoing 'art' project really. I exhibited pages from it
– as calligraphic works – in various galleries in the East End*

of London. By the time I was entering my final year, the novel existed in lots of different formats, and each one of them did something different.

For example?

Well, there was one that included photographs. Polaroids. And one where I decorated the pages in the style of an illuminated manuscript. As I say, Crocodilia *was more of an 'art gallery' piece than something for publication. But a lot of my fellow students – who enjoyed the actual story of it – kept telling me I should concentrate on that and try to get it published. In particular, my gay friends were very keen to get it into print. They thought it was a novel that could help young people.*

Because of the intense homophobia at the time?

'Intense homophobia' is an understatement. The LGBTQ community was being persecuted constantly. The concept of equal rights didn't seem to apply to us at all. Gay relationships were still illegal in many circumstances. The age of consent for homosexuals was much higher than for heterosexuals. We had a government in power – led by Margaret Thatcher – that was openly and virulently homophobic. Don't forget, it was Thatcher who said at a Party Conference that no young person had 'an inalienable right to be gay.' In other words, they had no right to be gay at all! And it was Thatcher who brought in Clause 28, which basically made it illegal for teachers to talk about homosexuality, unless it was in derogatory terms. Teachers lost their jobs just for saying they were gay. Gay clubs were being raided by police on a regular basis. Men were being stopped by police just for holding hands. I was stopped – Sorry, sorry. I'm ranting now.

Rant all you like.

The thing is this. When I was growing up I saw no real representation of LGBTQ people at all. Not one. Never. As far as I knew, I was the only teenager like me in the whole of East London. Perhaps the whole of London. I didn't know where and how to meet another gay man. I remember thinking that perhaps I wouldn't find anyone. Not ever. And, even if I did meet someone – what do I do? How do I start having a relationship with someone of the same sex? I had no idea! I had no role models. And so, in many ways, I wrote Crocodilia *as a . . . well, as the kind of novel I wish I could've read when I was young. A novel where being gay isn't questioned. Where it's not 'an issue'. It just . . . is.*

I don't think Dominic or Billy – or Dominic and Seb – even *talk* about homosexuality!

Why should they? Romeo and Juliet talk about a lot of things, but being heterosexual isn't one of them.

But it's not mentioned by any of the straight characters either.

That's right. Nothing needs to be explained or justified.

But weren't there people at the time who felt it was all a bit too much a . . . a . . .

A wish fulfilment fantasy? There were some who felt like that, yes. They thought it wasn't fully engaged with Gay Liberation battle. And I saw their point. Of course I did. I was as politically active as the rest of them. I went on every march. I talked about gay rights non-stop. I was out, proud, and very, very loud. And I'd experienced first-hand how much anger – often violence – that kind of outspokenness could provoke. Especially – especially – at that dreadful time for the gay community.

You're referring to AIDS.

I am. You know, I remember the exact moment I first heard someone make any reference to it. It was my best friend, Terry. We were walking down Charing Cross Road, and he said, 'Have you heard about this new thing that can kill us?'

When was this?

Oh . . . It must've been . . . late in 1981? I remember, for a long while after that, there didn't seem to be any useful, objective information about the virus at all. This was before the Internet, don't forget. If the mainstream media didn't publish anything . . . well, you were in the dark. And often, even when they did publish, you were still pretty much in the dark. All we knew was that there was this 'new thing', a virus, that was killing gay men and no one knew how you caught it. There were rumours, of course. Lots of them. It was caused by taking poppers. It was caused by mysterious fungus only found in gay clubs. It was caused by the FBI testing chemical weapons in San Francisco. And, of course, the tabloid press were having a field day. Headlines like 'GAY PLAGUE' and 'GOD'S WRATH ON HOMOSEXUALS'. They almost gleefully reported the rising number of gay men who had died. It was a terrible and a terrifying time. I still find it hard to talk about. And I find it almost impossible to write about. And yet . . .

And yet?

Well ... with Crocodilia *... it's strange, but ... I can sort of feel that time between the lines. It haunts the novel somehow.*

Can you say a bit more about that?

Oh ... the way Dominic is so determined to know more about Billy's previous lover, for example. Yes, of course, it's jealousy on Dominic's part. But at that time ... well, this need to know about a potential partner's sexual history – it obsessed all of us.

And there are several deaths in the novel.

Yes. A character dies in each of the story threads. But, as I say, all the 'darker' feelings and experiences of that time are between the lines. The lines themselves are, I hope, as bright and as sexy as the heatwave in which the story takes place.

And, surely, to publish a 'bright and sexy' novel like Crocodilia in the midst of what was happening back then ... well, that *was* a political act, right?

I always thought so, yes. This doesn't mean, of course, that I think we should ignore the horrors and injustices of the past. And the present. Yes, things have got a lot better. But there's still inequality and discrimination. There's still the micro-aggressions LGBTQ people experience every day. And in many places they aren't 'micro' at all. They're 'macro'. Russia, for instance, where things haven't got better at all. And in many countries homosexuality is still punishable by death. So we have a duty to remember all of this, to write about it, to talk about it, so that no one is ever able to ignore it or forget it. As the playwright August Wilson once said, 'To know who you are, and what you should be doing, you have to first know what your history is.' But, at the same time, we have to look to the future. We have to show how the world could be. Should be. We have to . . . envisage the rainbow, if you like.

And you wanted *Crocodilia* to be part of that envisaged rainbow.

Oh, I did. Very much.

And it could be said that if *Crocodilia* does the 'looking forward' thing, then your second novel, *In the Eyes of Mr Fury*, does the 'remembering' thing?

Yes, that's right. And I'd started writing Mr Fury *while I was finishing* Crocodilia. *So it helped me have the confidence to push each of those novels in their own particular direction.*

Was it difficult consolidating all the various 'formats' of *Crocodilia* into one publishable draft?

Not really. It was pretty clear what aspects of the novel would only really work in an art gallery setting. Once I'd discarded those it was just a case of refining it so that the narrative – or narratives – could shine as brightly as possible.

And then you sent it to a publisher?

I did. In the summer of 1983, I seem to remember. I sent it to Brilliance Books. One of those rarest of things at that time – a gay publishing house. Brilliance Books let me know very quickly that they wanted it. Which was wonderful news. What wasn't so wonderful is I had to wait about five years for it to be actually published. But these things happen, I guess.

What was the reaction when it was published?

Well, the sex scenes became a bit of a cause célèbre.

They can still raise an eyebrow.

Oh, good.

Didn't the novel become an underground phenomenon in Russia?

That's right! Someone there did a translation of it, had it secretly printed, and gave free copies to gay men. I was so proud of that. I still get very emotional when I think about it.

Can you say something about the further 'evolutions' you made to the novel for this brand-new edition?

Well, some of them were conceived during that five year hiatus before publication, but didn't make it – for various reasons – into that first published text. But the most important thing for this new edition is that I knew upfront the novel would have – for the first time! – all the different font styles it needed. Handwriting for all the various letters, a gothic style for the fairy tale, and a typewriter font for the family history sections. And also it would have the specific page layouts I had always requested. Knowing all this made all the difference. It enabled me to push the storyline intercutting in the way I'd always intended. Especially with the whole set-piece finale, where all the stories finally weave together.

You've referred to that section as a 'storytelling fugue'.

And it is. Sort of.

The opening line of the novel is, 'This is a story about crocodiles.' But it seems to me that it's really a story about stories, right?

Well, stories are at the heart of it, yes. The stories we tell to create ourselves. The stories we tell to create others. The stories we tell about the past. And, of course, the stories we tell to fall in love.

And the stories we tell to envisage the rainbow.

I hope so.